A smile tugged at one corner of his mouth,

but his eyes were calm.

All at once she felt light-headed. She couldn't look away from him.

Was it possible this stiff, unfriendly man had a glimmer of understanding about how she felt?

No, not possible. He planned to send his baby daughter—his own child—thousands of miles across the sea to Scotland. What kind of man would do that?

Still, he had kept her secret. And he hadn't objected—well, not too strongly, at least—when she'd spoken up about sending his child away.

Absentmindedly, Erika pressed new patterns into her mounded potatoes while she tried to think about the man who faced her across the table. Dr. Jonathan Callender held her future in the palm of his smooth, aristocratic hand. She had to try to understand him.

More than that, she had to please him...!

Dear Reader,

As the weather heats up this month, so do the passion and adventure in our romances!

Let's begin with handsome single father Dr. Jonathan Callender and his darling baby girl, who will undoubtedly warm your heart in *Plum Creek Bride,* an emotional new Western by Lynna Banning. Critics have described the author's works as "evocative," "touching" and "pure fun!" In this marriage-of-convenience tale, German nanny Erika Scharf arrives in Oregon to care for the Callender child, and finds a grieving widower who struggles to heal a town plagued by cholera. But it is Erika who heals Jonathan—by teaching him how to love again.

Medieval fans, prepare yourself for an utterly romantic forced-marriage story with Susan Spencer Paul's latest, *The Captive Bride,* about a fierce knight who'll stop at nothing to reclaim his family's estate—even marriage! Ana Seymour brings us *Lord of Lyonsbridge,* the daring tale of a sinfully handsome horse master who teaches a spoiled Norman beauty important lessons in compassion and love.

Temperatures—and tempers—flare in *Heart of the Lawman* by Linda Castle, which is set in Arizona Territory. Here, a single mother is released from prison, only to find that the man who mistakenly put her there, Sheriff Flynn O'Bannion, is awfully close to capturing her heart!

Whatever your tastes in reading, you'll be sure to find a romantic journey back to the past between the covers of a Harlequin Historicals® novel.

Sincerely,

Tracy Farrell
Senior Editor

Please address questions and book requests to:
Harlequin Reader Service
U.S.: 3010 Walden Ave., P.O. Box 1325, Buffalo, NY 14269
Canadian: P.O. Box 609, Fort Erie, Ont. L2A 5X3

PLUM CREEK BRIDE

Lynna Banning

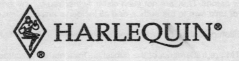

HARLEQUIN®

TORONTO • NEW YORK • LONDON
AMSTERDAM • PARIS • SYDNEY • HAMBURG
STOCKHOLM • ATHENS • TOKYO • MILAN • MADRID
PRAGUE • WARSAW • BUDAPEST • AUCKLAND

ISBN 0-373-29074-8

PLUM CREEK BRIDE

Copyright © 1999 by Carolyn Woolston

All rights reserved. Except for use in any review, the reproduction or utilization of this work in whole or in part in any form by any electronic, mechanical or other means, now known or hereafter invented, including xerography, photocopying and recording, or in any information storage or retrieval system, is forbidden without the written permission of the publisher, Harlequin Enterprises Limited, 225 Duncan Mill Road, Don Mills, Ontario, Canada M3B 3K9.

All characters in this book have no existence outside the imagination of the author and have no relation whatsoever to anyone bearing the same name or names. They are not even distantly inspired by any individual known or unknown to the author, and all incidents are pure invention.

This edition published by arrangement with Harlequin Books S.A.

® and TM are trademarks of the publisher. Trademarks indicated with ® are registered in the United States Patent and Trademark Office, the Canadian Trade Marks Office and in other countries.

Visit us at www.romance.net

Printed in U.S.A.

Books by Lynna Banning

Harlequin Historicals

Western Rose #310
Wildwood #374
Lost Acres Bride #437
Plum Creek Bride #474

LYNNA BANNING

has combined a lifelong love of history and literature into a satisfying new career as a writer. Born in Oregon, she has lived in Northern California most of her life, graduating from Scripps College and embarking on her career as an editor and technical writer, and later as a high school English teacher.

An amateur pianist and harpsichordist, Lynna performs on psaltery and recorders with two Renaissance ensembles and teaches music in her spare time. Currently she is learning to play the harp.

She enjoys hearing from her readers. You may write to her directly at P.O. Box 324, Felton, CA 95018.

For Suzanne Barrett.

With grateful thanks to Yvonne Woolston, Andrew and
Shirley Yarnes, Leslie Yarnes Sugai, Lawrence Yarnes
and my great-grandmother, Mareia Bruhn Boessen.

Chapter One

Plum Creek, Oregon, 1886

The searing July heat boiled up from the road as Erika gazed up the tree-shaded street. She shifted her heavy satchel to her other hand. She had walked all the way from the stagecoach stop, and the plain, high collar of her wilted travel dress stuck to her neck. Perspiration trickled between her breasts, and her feet, imprisoned in tight high-button shoes, baked like twin loaves of *Brot*. Bread, she corrected. English words were so hard to remember!

She turned up the street, trudged another twenty paces and stopped. The two-story house occupied the entire corner across from where she stood. A white board fence encircled the meticulously groomed emerald lawn, and a scrolled iron sign hung from a porch rafter. Jonathan Callender, Physician.

Such a grand home!

A trio of graceful plum trees shaded the huge gray-and-black Victorian structure from the merciless sun. Erika moved past the neat row of scarlet zinnias bordering the gravel path leading to the front porch, unlatched the gate and marched up the cobbled walk. Settling her satchel on the painted veranda floor, she lifted the iron knocker and rapped twice. After what seemed an interminable wait, she rapped again. Someone must be home; a dusty black buggy stood in front of the house.

Another long minute passed, and Erika tapped her foot in frustration.

Abruptly the door swung inward, and a tall, dark-haired man faced her. The sleeves of his rumpled white shirt were rolled up to his elbows, and the collar gaped open at the neck.

"Yes?" His rich, deep voice startled her with the impatiently clipped single word.

Erika swallowed. "My name Erika Scharf."

"Yes?" he repeated. Weary gray eyes surveyed her with disinterest.

"Name means no-thing?" She winced as she realized her pronunciation error. She had to work hard at English, but thoughts came faster than her tongue could form the words.

"Nothing at all. Should it?"

"You not get my letter? Your wife, Mrs...." She

extracted a slip of paper from her reticule and squinted at it. "Ben-bough?"

"Mrs. Benbow. My housekeeper."

"She write and— Oh! Your housekeeper? Not your wife?"

"That is correct. Now, Miss Scharf, perhaps you would tell me why your name should mean something to me?"

For some reason the look of the man made her feel hot and cold all at once. "Oh, yes, my name. My papa German. Mama she is—was—Danish. When I come New York, name not Scharf, but Scharffenberger. Too long to write, so they make short. Scharf. Is more American, *ja?*"

"*Ja.* Yes," Jonathan amended hastily.

"You do not remember name?"

"I do not." What did this chit of a girl want with him? Was she ailing?

"Are you ill, Miss Scharf?"

Two dimples appeared in her sunburned cheeks. "*Nein.* Never ill. Much health. I go to work now?"

"Work?" he echoed.

"*Ja,* work. W-o-r-k," she spelled. "Did not your wife tell you?"

"My wife is…" He could not bring himself to say it. "Tell me what?"

"Mrs. Ben-bough, Benbow, she write to me in

New York and say, 'Come to help, is baby coming.' There is baby, yes?''

Jonathan started. A shard of pain ripped into his belly. ''Yes, there is a baby.''

Tess must have sent for the young woman months ago. He had never been told.

''Come in, Miss Scharf.''

Erika stepped through the wide doorway. ''Baby is called...?''

''Marian. Marian Elizabeth.'' His throat tight, he ushered the young woman into the parlor.

''I will see house later,'' she said. She did not sit down, but flitted about the room inspecting everything—Tess's tall walnut harp, the settee she had ordered reupholstered in forest green velvet, the polished oak end table piled high with medical journals from the East, then the harp again. The young woman ran one finger over the dusty surface.

''I would like now to see my room, please.''

Jonathan jerked. ''Your room?''

''Yes, please. I come to stay, help with baby.''

Jonathan watched the slim young woman hoist her traveling bag and turn toward the wide mahogany staircase. Tess had not told him about the baby in the first place, and when she did, she hadn't admitted how risky it was for her. Now he found his wife had engaged a—a what? He already had a housekeeper. A mother's helper?

He groaned inwardly. Another surprise.

"You cannot remain here, Miss Scharf. My wife is... She passed away three weeks ago. There is no mother, and there is no need for a mother's helper."

"But there is baby!" Erika protested.

As if in corroboration, a thin wail drifted from behind a closed door. The honey-haired young woman stared at him accusingly.

"I come all the way from New York, from Bremerhaven on ship. I cannot go back. I have no money for ticket."

"I will pay your—"

"Besides," she interjected. "I do not *want* to go back. I like America. And Or-e-gon." She pronounced each syllable with care. "I like very much. So I do not go back." She folded her arms across her tiny waist and lifted her chin. "I stay."

"On the contrary, Miss Scharf. This is my house and my child. I can do whatever I feel necessary."

"But—"

"When the infant is six months old, I intend to send her to my mother in Scotland."

"You cannot," Erika exclaimed, her blue eyes widening. "Baby needs father."

Jonathan raked the fingers of one hand through his hair. "Baby needs—" He cleared his throat. "The child needs a mother. Someone to care for it, feed it. In Scotland—"

"In Scotland is not mother. *Or* father. Here in Plum Creek is family. You. Papa."

A smile flashed across her face, lighting the sapphire blue eyes from within. In the next instant, the curving lips pressed into a thin line and the sparkle in the wide-set eyes faded. "Next best thing to mama is mama's helper. Me. Erika Scharf."

She brushed past him, leaving the scent of lavender and travel dust in her wake. "I work now." She headed toward the staircase. "I will put on apron and then meet baby."

The doctor stepped forward. "You will not!"

Erika paused on the first polished riser. "And why not is that?" She suppressed a smile of triumph at so many correctly pronounced *w*'s today. She was learning! But the English came slowly.

Dr. Callender's hands closed into fists. "Is there something wrong with your hearing, Miss Scharf? I said I intend to send the child to Scotland."

"Nein." She met his gaze with an unflinching stare of her own. "Hearing good. Seeing also good. Thinking—" she tapped a forefinger against her forehead "—best of all! Baby stay here, with papa."

He drew himself up to his full height. "Now, look, miss. You may stay the night, and that is all. In my home, I decide what is best."

Erika tipped her head to meet his gaze. *"Ja,* of course," she agreed. "But baby not on Scotland ship now. Later maybe, not now. Now, baby is here. *I* am here. You—papa—are here. Is for the best, I think. You will see.''

She spun and started dragging the satchel up the stairs. "Which room, please? I put on apron now.''

Erika did not look back at him on purpose. She didn't want to give the frowning man at the bottom of the stairs one second to open his mouth and stop her ascent to what was surely the closest to heaven she'd ever been in her twenty-four years.

A house! A big, welcoming house, with beautiful furnishings and lace curtains at the windows—and so many windows, the glass sparkling clean, not dingy with soot as in her parents' tiny cottage at home. Mama would be so happy for her! Mama had always wanted a window.

A house in America! It was almost too good to be true. America... Land of the free, Papa had said. Where people were equal. It was all he'd talked about before he died. In America, even a poor German cobbler could eat.

More than that. An unmarried woman could work hard and save money, could stay respectable even if she did not marry. A young woman in America had a future.

And now that she was finally here, nothing—not fire or flood or Dr. Jonathan Callender—would keep her from starting her new life. It was what Papa had wanted for her. It was what *she* wanted. In fact, it was the only thing she wanted—to live in America.

She reached the last door in the long hallway and tentatively laid her hand on the polished brass knob. *This one?* she wondered. The door was smaller than the others.

Now at last she was here, at the home where she was needed. She quailed at her defiance of the formidable-looking physician, but she would never, ever give up her only offer of employment. Or her dream. And, she resolved, she would never, never admit how frightened she was.

She twisted the doorknob and walked in.

Erika stared at the lovely room. A Brussels carpet in tones of rose and burgundy spread over the floor, and on top of it, centered between two tall multi-paned windows, stood a narrow bed swathed in ivory lace. There were few other furnishings except for an imposing carved walnut chiffonier and a night table next to the bed. On it sat a white china basin and matching pitcher.

The small, simple room looked comfortable and inviting. It was sumptuous, by Erika's standards. Surely she must have opened the wrong door! Mrs. Callender had promised she would have her own room, but this—this seemed far too grand for a servant's quarters. This was luxury indeed, compared with the threadbare boardinghouses and dirty hotels she had occupied this past month of traveling from New York across the plains and mountains to Portland and then south to Plum Creek.

In spite of herself, she took a cautious step onto the richly patterned carpet. Mercy, her travel-stained shoes would surely soil it! Quickly she unhooked the laces, stepped out of the brown canvas shoes and edged onto the patterned carpet in her stocking feet. The thick, soft wool caressed her toes. What heaven!

Yes, it must be the wrong room. But so beautiful. So welcoming, as if waiting just for her. On impulse she slid one bureau drawer open. Empty.

She slid it closed and opened another. Empty, except for a spray of dried lavender scenting the flowered paper lining. If the room belonged to someone, would not the drawers be full? With a gasp of pleasure, she realized Mrs. Callender's intention: the room was to be Erika's!

She felt as if she had died and floated up to live with the angels. A room to herself! A private, quiet place where she could be alone! Never in her life had she had a door she could close to keep the world out.

And a bed covered in lace, like a wedding cake! She plunged her hands under the bedclothes. And a real mattress!

Hers! Her throat closed with emotion. Hurriedly she scrabbled in her satchel for the clean, white apron folded at the bottom and dumped the remaining contents into the open bureau drawer. The doctor had to let her stay! He had to!

With shaking hands she removed her straw hat and drew the apron neckband over her head, fashioning the ties into a wide bow at her waist. Smoothing out the sharp creases in the starched material, she surveyed herself in the oval mirror propped on the chiffonier.

She pinched her cheeks with both hands to make sure she wasn't dreaming, then reinserted a hairpin into the loose bun of honey-colored hair piled on top of her head. Tomorrow she would braid it into a crown as she had in the old country.

Hastily she flicked her cambric pocket handerchief over the dusty shoes and was bending to pull them on when a piercing cry penetrated the quiet.

Erika jerked upright. The baby. Casting a quick look at the pristine, feminine bedroom, she bolted for the door and pulled it shut behind her.

A lusty wail rose from below, punctuated by a man's impatient voice and the thump of footsteps as he apparently paced back and forth. Erika paused at the bottom of the stairs, consciously straightened her spine and drew in a fortifying breath. She was ready.

She moved toward the crying that rose from behind a closed door. Just as she lifted her hand to knock, the door jerked open.

"It's about time," the physician barked. "What the devil were you doing up there?"

Erika took an involuntary step backward. Perspiration beaded the doctor's high, tanned forehead. Tendrils of black hair curled awry, as if he had combed his fingers over his scalp. The penetrating gray eyes narrowed into shards of slate as he awaited her response.

"I was putting on my—"

"I can see that," he snapped. With a sigh he turned away, gesturing toward a wrinkled wraith of a woman in a severe black dress, seated beside an unadorned white wicker cradle.

"This is Mrs. Benbow, my housekeeper. Erika...what was it again? Ah, yes. Scharf. Erika Scharf."

The older woman fanned herself with one corner of a tea towel and pinned snapping black eyes on her. "What church are ye?" she demanded over the baby's cries.

"Church?" Did she dare admit she did not regularly attend church? All she knew was that the service was not conducted in Latin, so she could not be Catholic. "Why, Protestant, I suppose."

"You suppose? Don't you know? How were ye raised, if I might ask?"

"I was brought up in Germany," Erika replied, trying to keep her voice steady. "Papa Catholic.

Mama Lutheran.'' She did not add that her grandfather, her father's father, had been a Jew. Papa had
converted before he met Mama.

"Well, that's a fine muddle!'' The woman jostled
the edge of the wicker crib. "Hush now, child.''

Erika risked a peek into the cradle. A tiny pink
mouth stretched open, emitting screams of anguish.
At Erika's touch, the crying stopped abruptly, and
two startled, tear-filled blue eyes gazed up at her.

Mrs. Benbow sighed. "The wee thing's hungry.
Again,'' she added with a grimace.

Erika glanced at Dr. Callender, who had resumed
his pacing. The tall man tramped back and forth before a huge mahogany desk littered with papers and
journals.

"The child cries constantly,'' he growled. "Likely
cannot yet tolerate cow's milk. I cannot see patients
with all this din and uproar, and Mrs. Benbow cannot
cook and clean house and care for a child as well.
She must be sent to Scotland, and the sooner the
better.''

Mrs. Benbow nodded in agreement. "I canna
climb stairs any longer, so we have kept the bairn
down here, in doctor's study. But with my back the
way it is...'' Her voice trailed off.

The wailing resumed. Erika disengaged her forefinger from the baby's grasp. "May I pick her up?''

"Of course, of course,'' the old woman rasped.

"That's why ye've come, isn't it? Miss Tess had me send for ye. Not that I thought much o' the idea, but seein' as how things turned out, perhaps it's for the best."

Erika hesitated. She sensed the woman's resentment. She deduced that Mrs. Benbow had run the Callender household for some time. Erika's arrival was an obvious intrusion on the crusty housekeeper's territory.

"Well, go on!" the older woman rasped. "Pick the babe up and get her to stop crying, if ye can."

Erika reached into the cradle and slid her hands under the blanketed bundle. Lifting her up, she held the infant securely against her body. The tiny creature lay warm and fragrant on her breast. A sweet, soapy fragrance rose from her skin.

Erika's heart squeezed. The baby was exquisite, like a porcelain doll with her fair skin and rosy cheeks and huge blue eyes. And so tiny! So perfectly formed!

"Mrs. Callender must have very beautiful been," she murmured.

The doctor turned away abruptly. Erika watched as he bent his head and fingered a framed portrait on his cluttered desk.

"Aye, she was that," Mrs. Benbow volunteered with a significant look at her employer. "'Tis a sad house ye've come to, lass. Nothing's been the same since Miss Tess has been gone.''

Erika saw the doctor turn the photograph face down on his desk, but still he did not turn around. A silence thick as cold molasses descended as Mrs. Benbow dabbed at her eyes with the towel.

Erika waited for someone to speak. After a long minute, she concluded that the conversation had come to an end.

The baby's comforting weight against her breast reminded her why she had come in the first place—to help with the infant. Now more than ever she wanted to stay and work in this house with its spacious, elegantly arranged rooms and the lacy, private bedroom upstairs. More than that, she realized, she felt an inexorable pull toward the soft bundle snuggled in her arms.

"I presume you will leave in the morning," the doctor announced. His voice sounded ragged with fatigue. The expression in his face was cold, as if a lifeless mask had been drawn over his features. But in his eyes, Erika saw the agony of a bereaved man and a silent, unconscious cry for help.

She shifted the baby to her shoulder. "I stay for three dollar a week," she said quietly.

"No," the physician said. "Mrs. Benbow can manage until—"

Mrs. Benbow slapped the tea towel onto her lap. "I say she's a gift from God."

"No," Dr. Callender repeated.

The housekeeper studied Erika with unsmiling eyes. "She's young, but she'll do in a pinch."

The doctor scowled.

"Just until—Lord preserve us, lass!" the housekeeper cried. "Where are your shoes?"

Erika winced. In her haste, she'd forgotten them.

Fighting back a choking fear, she caught Dr. Callender's cool, calculating gaze as he awaited her answer. Would he dismiss her on the spot for being a lackwit?

"Well, Miss Scharf?" His tone was silky with derision.

"I—" A warm wetness seeped through the soft blanket. "The baby is needful," she said, quickly shifting the topic.

She bent over the cradle and laid the infant on its back. Reaching for the diaper folded over the foot of the crib, she spoke over her shoulder. "I stay. Shoes do not matter."

Erika lifted the square of soft cotton diaper and froze. She knew nothing about babies! She was a cobbler's daughter, the only child Mama and Papa ever had. She'd never even had any younger cousins to care for. Oh, what was she to do?

She knew what a diaper was for, but how in the

world was it attached? She'd been engaged to do laundry and ironing, maybe watch over the child when the mama went out. But now she was not the helper—she was the mama!

She felt eyes boring into her back—one pair black and disapproving, one pair gray and distant. Measuring.

Erika closed her eyes and uttered a brief, silent prayer. *Help me, God! Show me about diapers!*

When she opened her lids, the room hummed with tension. Summoning her courage, Erika unfolded the diaper and peeked under the infant's soaked cambric gown.

Chapter Two

With grudging admiration, Jonathan watched as Erika bent over the wicker cradle. She wasn't the first serving girl to be subjected to Adeline Benbow's assessing eye and pointed questions, but she was the first to stay more than five minutes after the experience.

How long Miss Scharf would last under his housekeeper's exacting rule was another matter entirely, but at the moment the prospect solved the problem of what to do with the young woman. Since Mrs. Benbow expressed a preference for the girl's help, however temporary, he couldn't simply turn her out.

He'd lay odds she'd last less than a week. Mrs. Benbow could be a stern taskmaster, and now that she was too old to climb the stairs more than once a day, she bore an extra grudge against life in general and young women in particular. If Miss Scharf lasted more than the week, he'd try to find her another position. But she would need the hide of a rhinoceros to survive even one day under Mrs. Benbow.

He watched Erika gently lift the folds of the cambric sacque away from the baby's body with capable, graceful hands. The look on her face when she touched his daughter told him she had a sentimental nature. And sentiment meant vulnerability. If he knew anything about women, Miss Scharf had a soft heart, and because of it, she would suffer. In spite of himself, he felt a twinge of sympathy for the eager, rosy-cheeked woman.

Erika smoothed out the diaper and draped it over the edge of the wicker cradle. Moving very deliberately, she unsnapped the safety pins holding the wet garment in place. As she did so, she studied the arrangement of folds in the material, the position of the fasteners, how they were attached. With care, she lifted away the wet diaper.

The housekeeper watched her every move, then tossed the tea towel she'd been fanning herself with into the cradle. Erika's toes curled. What was she supposed to do with *that?*

"Cornstarch is in the candy dish," the older woman offered in a dry tone. She pointed to a fluted glass bowl on a side table.

Cornstarch? Why would she need cornstarch?

As if in answer to her unspoken question, Dr. Callender spoke in a low, controlled voice. "It is much superior to nursery powder."

Powder! Of course. With an inward sigh of relief, she rolled the wet diaper into a wad and deposited it on an empty corner of the doctor's desk. She heard Mrs. Benbow's snort of disapproval and the physician's quick intake of breath, but she was too distracted to care. Cornstarch must be for the baby's moist skin. She eyed the huck tea towel.

That was it! She must dry the infant's tender skin, then dust on the fine white powder. *Oh, thank you, God, for showing me how to proceed.*

She snatched up the wrinkled towel and just as quickly discarded it. "Is soiled," she said as calmly as she could. "May I have clean one?"

The housekeeper rose and drew herself up with an air of superiority. The stiff bombazine dress rustled in the quiet room, and Erika had a quick vision of a peacock displaying its feathers.

"Certainly," the woman snapped. The door clicked shut behind her.

Left alone with the doctor, Erika experienced a moment of panic. Would he notice her inexperience?

She kept her back to him as she folded the dry material into what she judged to be a diaper-shaped rectangle. The door opened and in swept Mrs. Benbow, a clean towel in her hand. Erika accepted it, then reached for the dish of cornstarch. She patted the baby's damp skin with the towel, then dusted on the powder with the cotton ball in the dish cover.

As she lifted the folded diaper she managed a surreptitious glance behind her. Both Dr. Callender and his housekeeper had their attention riveted on her. She could block out one person's view with her body, but not both. One of them would just have to witness her first fumbling attempt at changing an infant's diaper. Which one should it be?

She chose the housekeeper. The physician would dismiss her at once if he suspected how inexperienced she was. Mrs. Benbow might disapprove, but she would not complain, since she obviously regarded caring for the infant herself with some distaste.

Keeping her back toward Dr. Callender, Erika lifted the baby's tiny legs and slid the material beneath her rump. She wished her hands would stop shaking! Slowly she brought the material up between the kicking limbs. Praying she would not stab the infant with the pin, she forced the point through thicknesses of cotton material and, using her finger as a guide, snapped the device securely in place. When the second pin closed, Erika breathed in relief. She'd done it!

"Humph!" Mrs. Benbow sniffed behind her. "Now I s'pose you'll need that milk heated up. I'll have to go poke up my stove.'' With a sour look on her face, the woman yanked open the study door.

''Please,'' Erika was amazed to hear herself say. ''Pour out old milk. Use fresh.''

The housekeeper stiffened, and Erika held her breath.

''Miss Scharf is right,'' the doctor said in a low, even voice. ''In this hot weather, milk clabbers readily.''

''Harrumph!'' The housekeeper huffed and swished away, an angry set to her thin, hunched shoulders.

Milk, Erika thought desperately. Babies needed milk, of course, but how much? How warm? And if not from a mother's breast, how was it to be drunk?

''Boil the nursing flask, too, Mrs. Benbow,'' the physician called through the open door.

Ah, that was it—a bottle of some sort! Erika covered her relief by lifting the infant into her arms. Except for a single blanket over the mattress, no other bedding softened the bare wicker.

She stared down at the starkly appointed cradle, then pivoted toward the doctor. ''Where is kept baby's clothes and...bed makings?''

''Tess...'' A momentary flash of anguish twisted the physician's regular features. He swallowed, then continued. ''My wife stored the baby's things in the nursery.''

"Nursery? Where is nursery?"

"Upstairs. Mrs. Benbow cannot manage the stairs, so she moved the cradle into my study until...for the time being."

"I move back to nursery," Erika announced. "I can go up and down stairs. I t'ink is why missus send for me."

Jonathan said nothing. He strode to the lace-shrouded window, drew the panel to one side and stared out. He would be glad to have the child ensconced out of earshot in the special room Tess had insisted on when she had finally confessed her pregnancy. Every sound the baby made reminded him of his wife's untimely death. Even so, he wasn't sure he wanted to be left alone with himself in the sanctuary of his study.

But life could not stop because Tess was gone. It was time for him to see patients again. He had to resume his practice, or that quack Chilcoate would kill off half the town.

"Yes, move the babe upstairs," he said, clipping his words short. *And as for you, Erika Scharf, stay out of my sight.*

To be honest, he wanted nothing to do with Tess's child, or the young woman she had engaged without telling him. Women, he had learned, were devious and dishonest. Never again, he resolved, would he allow himself to love one. No woman would ever again enchain his heart.

And no child, either.

Erika frowned as she inspected the nursery. The small, stifling room next to her own chamber smelled of dust and dried lavender and obviously had never been used. A stack of clean diapers filled the lace-ruffled bassinet; on top of the broad, waist-high chest on the opposite wall lay a folded blue knit shawl. A cobweb looped from the garment to one drawer pull.

A rocking chair stood next to the single window. Erika noticed the layer of dust between the dark walnut slats. It looked as if no one had ever sat in it.

She lifted the diapers off the striped ticking mattress and set them on top of the chest. God in heaven, the infant's bed had not even been made up!

Erika cocked her head to one side. The untouched state of the room answered her questions about the odd situation she'd stepped into. From birth, the child had evidently been cared for by the housekeeper— fed and tended to in the wicker cradle downstairs in the doctor's study. Considering Mrs. Benbow's spare, bent frame, her inability to climb the stairs and her obvious reticence about picking up the baby even when it wailed, Erika surmised the child had received attention only out of duty. Even the papa, Dr. Callender, seemed uninterested. Remote.

Had he delivered the infant and immediately relegated her to the care of his dour housekeeper as his wife lay dying? Poor man.

And the poor *Liebchen!* What a sad beginning for a child. No one to hold or comfort her, no warm mama's body to nestle against, no breast to suckle. Erika knew instinctively what the child needed. Love.

And that silent, enigmatic man whose house this was planned to send his own child to Scotland? Erika would die first. The instant those tiny, perfect pink fingers had curled around her thumb, Erika's heart had contracted. Now the child lay downstairs, looked after but not loved. It was not good enough.

She plucked the handerchief from her apron pocket and whisked it over the dusty chair and bureau top, shook out the shawl and folded the mound of diapers and laid them in an empty drawer. In the middle drawer she found a set of infant-sized sheets and a tiny pillowcase with embroidered pink and gold flowers twining around the edge. She made up the bassinet, laid a rose-edged crocheted baby blanket over the top sheet and opened the window to air the room. A warm, sweet-scented breeze washed over her perspiring face.

Erika pressed her forefinger against the smooth rocker back, setting it in motion. *Forgive me if I not know everything, Mrs. Callender, but I learn quick. I will take good care of your beautiful baby girl.*

She watched the chair tip slowly forward and then back on its long, curved runners, as if nodding in silent agreement.

Chapter Three

Chapter Three

Erika slipped the cambric sacque over the baby's head and cradled the tiny form in the crook of her arm. In the single day since her arrival in Plum Creek, she had mastered not only changing diapers but dressing and feeding Marian Elizabeth Callender. Now, alone in the kitchen on Sunday morning while Mrs. Benbow attended church, Erika planned to bathe the child for the first time.

Grateful not to have the housekeeper's sharp eyes assessing her every motion, she moved about the spotless, meticulously arranged pantry searching for a vessel to serve as the baby's bathtub. The teakettle on the stove hissed as she scanned the cabinets and long, painted shelves for a basin of the appropriate size.

Skillets, cooking pots of various sizes, three sets of china. What riches! She gazed about her in awe.

So many beautiful things! The blue-flowered plates she recognized from last night's dinner, eaten in haste on the small kitchen table while Mrs. Benbow grudgingly rocked the baby in the wicker cradle.

Aside from her own bedroom upstairs, the well-kept kitchen with its ornate, nickel-trimmed iron stove and the wealth of utensils and china and glassware was her favorite room.

Ah, there! On the top shelf! Her gaze fell upon a large white china bowl with a matching cover. Just the right shape for a baby to sit in, and the cover so clever—to keep the water warm until bath time! Shifting the infant to her other arm, Erika reached over her head to retrieve the basin.

Zu hoch. Too high up, she amended in English. She must remember to speak the language of America! She would never become a citizen of this great country if she could not.

Undaunted, she settled the infant on a folded towel in the oblong porcelained iron sink and dragged a stool over to the shelf. She climbed onto the stool and with care lifted down the curious dish, cover and all. At the same instant the tall figure of Dr. Callender filled the doorway.

His white shirt was rumpled, his eyes red rimmed, as if he had not slept. The tumble of unruly coal-black curls over his forehead gave him an almost jaunty, boyish look. But his pale, strained face told her otherwise.

"Good day, Miss Scharf. I thought I would brew myself a cup of tea before Mrs. Benbow..." He turned somber gray eyes up at her, perched on the stool, and his brows rose. "...returns from her weekly religious indulgence," he finished after a moment's hesitation.

"Water is hot," Erika said as she stepped off the stool. She set the china basin on the sideboard.

His gaze followed her, the expression on his face changing as he spied the infant. "What, may I ask, is the baby doing in the sink?"

"Oh, I bath baby now." Erika gestured at the covered dish. "I find, how you say, bath-ing tub, on shelf. You use first hot water in kettle to make tea, then I wash baby."

The eloquent, dark brows drew together. "You're going to bathe my daughter in *that?*"

"Is what Mrs. Benbow uses, *ja?*"

"Certainly not. This, young woman—" he tapped a deliberate forefinger on the dish cover "—is a soup tureen. A wedding gift from my wife's uncle in Savannah."

"Ah. I see."

Jonathan saw a sheepish smile curve the corners of her mouth.

"I make mistake."

He watched her hand dive into her apron pocket and withdraw a small notebook and a chewed pencil stub.

"How you spell, please?"

He spelled out the words slowly as she scribbled on the pad. "Toor-een," she pronounced. "For *Suppe, ja?*"

"For soup, yes. Not for bathing."

"Ah." The blue eyes sparkled with the joy of comprehension. "What for baby, then?"

Jonathan opened his mouth to reply, then snapped his jaw shut. He hadn't the faintest idea. To his surprise, it annoyed him, not knowing. He liked to have answers—remedies—for the problems that came his way. His lack of a ready solution in this area made him uneasy, as if a part of his life were drifting out of his control. What *would* one use to bathe the infant?

When he'd delivered newborns in other households, particularly those far from town, he'd used a bucket or a small washtub, whatever was handy and reasonably clean. He realized suddenly that after Tess's death he hadn't been interested enough in the child to wonder about her care.

The child's birth had cost him his wife. He had wanted nothing to do with Tess's child. He knew he should feel ashamed of such antipathy toward his own flesh and blood, but what he felt was not shame but rage. His soul was dead. His heart was fired not by love but by fury.

What a reprehensible man he must be underneath the veneer of good manners and education! He wasn't fit to lick the boots of the poorest, most illiterate farmer in Jackson County.

He wondered about himself, about his sanity. Because of Erika Scharf's question, because of her very presence in his kitchen at this moment, he felt himself jolted into a different awareness, as if he'd been sleeping and she had shaken him awake. Their roles were reversed. She belonged; he did not.

Great Scott, he was a stranger in his own house!

Erika pointed to the top shelf of a glass-fronted cabinet. "That one," she said, satisfaction tingeing her voice. "Reach for me, please?"

Jonathan eyed the stack of china plates and bowls. Extending one arm above her head, he opened the cabinet door and lifted down the indicated bowl. Tess's best Haviland vegetable dish. With suppressed amusement he handed the dish to the young woman who waited, arms outstretched.

He watched Erika run her fingers over the dish and bit back a chuckle. Mrs. Benbow prepared dinner each Sunday evening; tonight's meal might prove more interesting than usual. What would his housekeeper say when she discovered Erika's use for her favorite serving dish?

* * *

Erika smoothed her hands over the material of her best skirt, a simple gored blue percale that had seen many washings. It was her only other garment besides a serviceable denim work skirt and her black travel ensemble. She'd ironed out the creases earlier that afternoon, after the baby's bath and afternoon feeding, heating up the sadiron on the kitchen stove while she washed and dried the flowered china bowl she'd used for the baby's bath.

Now, with the infant sleeping soundly in the next room, she tucked the stray wisps of hair into the crown of braids she'd wound on top of her head, keeping one ear attuned to the nursery. She had purposely left the door ajar to hear if the child cried.

Her hand stilled. She had actually been invited to join the doctor and Mrs. Benbow in the dining room—not as a servant, but as if she were a member of the family. Once each week, the housekeeper had instructed, on the Lord's Day, Dr. Callender and his wife insisted the housekeeper join them at the formal Sunday meal. Now that his wife had "passed over," as the older woman put it, Dr. Callender wished to carry on the tradition. Erika would join them at the table.

She peeked into the nursery to satisfy herself that the baby still slept. At the sight of the delicate, perfect fingers curled outside the rose coverlet, her heart

38 *Plum Creek Bride*

lifted in her chest like a balloon. At any moment she expected to float up off the floor. A baby was a miracle from another world, so small and beautifully formed. She shook her head in wonder.

Downstairs, an ivory damask cloth covered the walnut table, which was laden with sparkling crystal and gleaming plates and bowls. Erika quailed at the sight. All those shiny forks and spoons, and glasses and plates on top of plates. How would she ever know which to use?

At the head of the table Dr. Callender sat, tapping a well-manicured forefinger against his crystal wineglass. Instead of the rumpled white shirt, the physician wore dark trousers and a black jacket, a silver-gray silk cravat loosely knotted under his chin. He looked every inch a prince, or even a king. And he was not smiling.

At his right, Mrs. Benbow perched stiffly in the high-backed chair like a black sparrow with sharp, unblinking eyes.

Erika's throat constricted. She hadn't the slightest notion what to say to the doctor, or to the formidable woman who stared at her with obvious disapproval.

"Miss Scharf." The doctor's low, unemotional voice sent a butterfly skittering into her stomach.

"In this house, meals are attended with unfailing punctuality."

Erika shifted her gaze from the housekeeper to the

dark-haired man at the head of the table. "What means that, unfailing punc—punctu...?"

"You're late," snapped the housekeeper. "That's what it means. My mashed potatoes will be stone-cold." She gestured at the mounded bowl on which a chunk of butter the size of a hen's egg melted.

"So sorry," Erika murmured as she slipped into the empty chair across from the stern-faced woman. "Baby cry and cry after the milk I give her. I could not sooner come."

"Quieting a crying child is a labor of Sisyphus," the doctor observed. "It never stops."

"I stop it," Erika said softly. "I rock her until crying stops, and she falls asleep. Cannot be very good mama if not have—how you say?—waiting. No, patience—that is the word! Patience."

The flicker of a smile twitched across the doctor's finely proportioned lips. "Patience," he echoed. He pushed back his chair and rose. "Cow's milk often does not agree with infants. Goat's milk might be better. Mrs. Benbow, help yourself to the vegetables while I carve."

Goat's milk! Where in the world would she find a goat? Erika opened her mouth to ask, but Dr. Callender lifted the cover off the serving platter and busied himself with a wickedly sharp-looking knife.

A tingle of apprehension danced up Erika's spine as she watched the physician's long, capable fingers expertly pare thin slices of roast chicken into a neat fan-shaped pile on the china platter. His quick, purposeful movements made her breath catch. He made cutting up the fowl look so simple, even graceful, as if he enjoyed slicing into the succulent flesh of a once-living creature.

Her heartbeat hiccuped. Of course, she reminded herself. He was *Dr.* Callender. Maybe he was also a surgeon, used to cutting into…things.

She shuddered and cast a look at the housekeeper. Mrs. Benbow's gaze followed every motion the physician made, an approving gleam in her eyes. No doubt she considered it *her* chicken, Erika thought, which she had prepared and offered up as a sort of sacrifice to her employer.

"White meat or dark?" the doctor inquired.

Erika blinked. "What?"

He studied her with quizzical gray eyes, the knife in one hand, a two-pronged silver fork in the other. "Breast or thigh?"

She couldn't utter a word. She hadn't the faintest idea. In all her twenty-four years she had never been asked such a question. It was either food or no food, never what *kind* of food; his question was beyond her understanding. She had so much to learn in America!

One thing she did know, however, was that speaking the word *breast* out loud in this man's presence was an impossibility. Already she felt her cheeks flame at the thought of such an intimacy. *Thigh* was just as bad.

"White," she choked out at last.

"Breast, then," he said. His voice was unemotional, but deep in his eyes a light flickered, as if he were secretly amused. "Mrs. Benbow?"

He lifted a generous piece of chicken onto Erika's plate as he waited for the housekeeper's reply.

"Chest, thank-ee."

The doctor chuckled. He served the housekeeper, then himself, taking both thigh and drumstick and a double spoonful of the fluffy whipped potatoes.

Erika mentally inscribed the word *chest* in her study notebook. She had thought it meant a piece of furniture with drawers, but in English, she was learning, one word could have two meanings. Repeating the word over and over in her head, she watched Mrs. Benbow dip the serving spoon into the oversize vegetable dish.

When it came her turn, she dug in the silver spoon and hesitated. The bowl looked familiar. She plopped the potatoes onto her plate, continuing to study the container.

It was the baby's bathtub! Erika froze in horror. Not two hours ago, she had used the same bowl to bathe the infant! What would Mrs. Benbow say if she knew?

But she *didn't* know, Erika assured herself. The sour-faced woman was totally absorbed in cutting her chicken "chest" into tiny square pieces. The housekeeper would only know about Erika's earlier use of the bowl if—

Her breath squeezed off. *If Dr. Callender told her!* Oh, dear God. Would he? Was her employment in America to last just these two magical days before she'd be turned out of this house to fend for herself?

Her heart in her throat, she sneaked a look at the black-haired, elegantly attired gentleman at the head of the table. Calmly he glanced at the vegetable dish and lifted a morsel of chicken past his lips. He chewed for what seemed an eternity, swallowed, then opened his mouth to speak.

Erika flinched as his gaze met hers. Now. He would tell Mrs. Benbow now what she had done with the vegetable bowl.

"Mrs. Benbow?"

The housekeeper bobbed her gray head. "Yes, sir?"

Erika shut her eyes. She didn't want to see the look on Mrs. Benbow's face when he told her.

"My compliments. This chicken is excellent."

"Why, thank you, sir!"

Erika's lids snapped open. Across the table a pair of gray eyes surveyed her with a keen look. One dark brow rose in a sardonic arch. "Is something wrong, Miss Scharf?" he inquired, his voice bland.

"No," Erika managed. She stabbed her fork into the potatoes on her plate, nervously moving them into a circle. She kept her eyes glued to the crisscross marks her fork tines made. "Nothing is wrong."

When at last she raised her head, she found he was still looking at her. A smile tugged at one corner of his mouth, but his eyes were the same—calm, distant, except for that sudden odd light in their depths.

All at once she felt as if her head was full of sunshine. She couldn't look away from him.

What was he thinking at this moment? Why had he not told Mrs. Benbow about the vegetable bowl?

Was it possible this stiff, unfriendly man had a glimmer of understanding about how she felt?

No, not possible. He planned to send his baby daughter—his own child—thousands of miles across the sea to Scotland. What kind of man would do that?

Still, he had kept her secret. And he hadn't objected—well, not too strongly, at least—when she'd spoken up about sending his child away.

Absentmindedly, Erika pressed new patterns into her potatoes while she tried to think about the man who faced her across the table. Dr. Jonathan Callender held her future in the palm of his smooth, aristocratic hand. She had to try to understand him.

More than that, she had to please him!

Chapter Four

Erika gave the goat's lead a determined tug. "Come, Jasmine! Doctor say goat milk good for baby. We will be late for feeding!"

The goat lifted its head from a cluster of pink roses twining over a picket fence and stopped chewing. Two hard black eyes regarded her with curiosity for a full minute before Erika gave another sharp jerk on the rope. The animal trotted after her.

Jubilant, she marched along Chestnut Street with a spring to her step. She had bargained for the goat at the first farm she'd reached on the road out of town, trading the promise of a free consultation with Dr. Callender for the best milk goat of the bemused farmer's herd. But getting the animal from the farmer's field to the doctor's backyard wasn't so easy.

So far, Jasmine had devoured most of the wild iris

blooms scattered along the road back to town, plus a large portion of a purple butterfly bush arching over a neighbor's fence, and now the roses. Erika sighed. Just a few more blocks, and she could tether the headstrong animal to the plum tree behind Dr. Callender's stable. With its preference for a diet of flowers, the milk should be extra rich and tasty!

Pleased, she tugged the animal around the corner onto Maple Street and tied it to the plum tree behind the whitewashed barn.

Jonathan lunged into the dusty black buggy, grabbed the reins and flicked them smartly over the mare's broad back. "Of all the confounded, muddle-headed arrogance," he muttered. "One of these days, so help me, I will throttle that quack Chilcoate within an inch of his life!"

Daisy leapt forward and trotted down Main Street. When the doctor forgot to signal his intention, the horse turned the corner by habit.

No, Jonathan amended, belatedly pulling on Daisy's rein. He would not throttle the man. He'd let the fool hang himself with his own rope. Sooner or later it had to happen; one of his noxious elixirs would poison someone. Jonathan prayed nightly for the health of the unwitting townspeople of Plum Creek and carried an extra bottle of ipecac in his medical bag.

Underneath, he knew getting rid of the incompetent old man wasn't going to change a thing. It was the mayor—that idiot banker, Brumbaugh—and the rest of his town council toadies who were bent on ignoring the situation until it would be too late. An hour ago he'd argued himself blue in the face, ended up shouting at the mayor and telling Rutherford Chilcoate to shut up unless he could speak intelligently or even comprehend the existence of bacteria.

What would it take to convince them he knew what he was talking about? They needed a new water system, one that bypassed contamination sources and had a reservoir and modern filtering equipment. Cholera had been rampant in eastern cities for the past decade; it was only a matter of time before it hit Plum Creek. A sixth sense told him it would be sooner rather than later, since the farms and small ranches upstream continued to let their animal waste matter seep into the town water supply. Summer would be hot. And long.

He flapped the mare's reins. Unfortunately, new water systems cost money. He'd offered to finance the project himself if they'd just vote on it! Their lack of concern made him so mad he could eat thistles.

He jerked the reins unnecessarily. Daisy had already halted in front of his house. Jonathan raked one hand through his hair, rose to step out of the buggy and stopped short. What in God's name had happened to the scarlet zinnias Tess had planted a month ago? Every single bloom in the carefully tended border had been nipped off at the crown.

He dropped the reins, bounded out of the buggy and strode up the walkway onto the veranda.

"Mrs. Benbow!" He surged through the front door and headed for the dining room.

The housekeeper poked her head out of the kitchen. "Sir? Why, whatever be the matter?"

"The zinnias! What happened to Tess's zinnias?"

Mrs. Benbow looked blank. "What's wrong with them?"

Jonathan strove to calm his breathing. "They're gone, that's what. No blooms, just stalks."

The housekeeper's eyes widened, then narrowed in comprehension. "Best ask Miss Scharf."

"Miss Scharf?" He barked the name. "What does Miss Scharf have to do with the zinnias?"

"Well," the old woman began, "it's not exactly her, it's probably…"

Jonathan pivoted and headed for the stairs before the housekeeper could finish her sentence. He went up two at a time and with the knuckle of his fisted hand gave a short, sharp rap on Erika's closed door.

"Miss Scharf?"

No answer. He knocked again, then edged the door open.

The room was empty. The lacy coverlet had been neatly drawn up on the bed, the single window propped wide open. A fresh, sweet-scented breeze ruffled the lace curtains. Jonathan paused, his hand resting on the doorknob.

Something felt different. The room was serene. Straightforward. No perfume atomizers or jewel boxes or other fripperies adorned the chest of drawers, no petticoats or discarded wrappers were tossed carelessly across the chair or the narrow bed. The faint smell of lemon oil made him lift his nose and sniff the air. For a moment he forgot the anger that had propelled him up the stairs.

Something about the room slammed a fist into his solar plexus. It was neat, well-ordered, purposeful, like its occupant—the single-minded young woman Tess had engaged as a helper.

Tess had never returned a garment to her capacious wardrobe or polished a single piece of furniture in her short married life.

That was it! The room seemed strange because it was not like Tess. In the next instant an ache laced his heart into a knot of anguish.

She's gone, you fool! Let her rest in peace.

His anger returned threefold. Someone had decimated the zinnia border Tess had wanted. Each morning for a week she had supervised the digging and planting undertaken by their neighbor, Theodore

Zabersky. Each morning for a week Tess had smiled at Jonathan instead of complaining about the long hours he spent seeing patients or all-night ordeals delivering babies on remote farms throughout the county.

It had been a sweet time for the two of them; he damn well wasn't going to let this reminder of it be destroyed!

He banged the door shut. "Miss Scharf?" He shouted her name louder than he'd intended. "Answer me!"

"Here," a muffled voice sounded. "In library."

Library? He didn't *have* a library. She must mean the upstairs sitting room. It was the only room in the house besides his study where Tess had allowed his books. What in God's name was an uneducated immigrant girl doing in there? He strode down the hallway and threw open the door.

Erika looked up from the desk—*his* desk, he noted with annoyance—and gave him a shy smile. The curve of her mouth faltered as he loomed over her.

"I—I hope you not mind," she said with a slight stammer. "I find quiet place for study." She indicated the notebook spread before her, flanked by a dictionary and a worn-looking textbook. "I pronounce new American words and write many times to remember."

Reading upside down, he made out a row of care-

fully penciled words. *Tureen.* Another line began
with *unerring* and ended with *congratulate.*

"Miss Scharf, what happened to the zinnia border?"

Her blue eyes widened. "Zinnia? What is zinnia,
please?" She lifted her pencil, poised it over the
notebook.

Jonathan clenched his jaw and counted to fifteen
before he trusted himself to speak. "Zinnias, my dear
young woman, are the flowers that grow along the
front path. Or did. Come here and take a look!" He
tramped over to the window.

When she joined him, he pulled aside the curtain
and directed her gaze to the walkway below.

"Flowers gone," she observed. She looked at him
expectantly.

"I'll say they're gone. The question, Miss Scharf,
is *where* have they gone? And why? In this household, you do not pick flowers without permission."

"But I do not pick!" she protested. "Maybe Mrs.
Ben—"

She halted, clapped one hand over her mouth for
a moment. "Oh! It was Jasmine! The goat."

"Goat!" Jonathan stared at her. "I don't have
a—"

But Erika was already heading for the doorway.
"Must have got loose, maybe eat rope!"

She flew ahead of him down the stairs, through

the kitchen and out the back door. Mrs. Benbow, stirring soup at the stove, paused with her spoon in midair.

"Excuse us," Jonathan panted as he strode past her.

Erika disappeared around the corner of the barn. By the time he caught up with her, she was yanking a small white goat with a frayed rope around its neck toward the plum tree. When she had secured the animal, she turned to face him.

"Goat bad for flowers, maybe. But is good for milk."

"Where did that animal come from?" he demanded.

"From farmer. Mr. Peck. He give."

"He *gave* it to you?" At her nod, he jammed his hands into his trouser pockets to keep from hitting something. "I don't believe it. Cyrus Peck never gave away anything free in his life."

"Not for free," Erika protested. "For—how you say—ex...ex...for trade."

Incredulous, Jonathan stared at her. "Trade for what?" he snapped.

"Trade one goat for one doctor visit. We get milk for baby, he get leg fixed."

"Leg fixed! There's nothing wrong with Cyrus Peck's leg that a little hard work wouldn't remedy."

The anger he'd tamped down inside him leapt to life. Cold fury washed through his veins.

"Do you mean to tell me you took it upon yourself to bring a goat, a destructive, messy animal, onto my property? Let it eat my wife's zinnia border? Let it—"

"I not let eat!" Erika's eyes blazed the color of a hot summer sky. "Goat get loose, eat rope. Eat... zinnias," she admitted. "I am sorry for flowers, but goat give good milk. I feed baby and not one crying. So is good," she announced. She raised her chin in defiance.

Jonathan didn't know whether to laugh or swear. Rage and amusement battled his brain to a standstill. Part of him wanted to strangle the young woman who stood before him.

She twisted her blue work skirt in both hands, then suddenly straightened her spine and drew herself up to her full height. The top of her head just reached his chin.

"Milk more important than flowers," she said in a determined voice. She tipped her head up and gave him a level look. "As papa, you want good for baby. As doctor, you say not cow's milk but goat milk good for her, so I get goat. I want good for baby, too!"

"Then keep the damn thing tied up!"

"*Ja,* I will," she said quietly. "Will also fix flowers."

"Everything has been topsy-turvy since you set foot in the door," Jonathan grumbled. "I ought to send you back to New York or Hamburg or wherever it is you came from."

Erika lifted her chin and surveyed him with steady blue eyes. "I stay in America. I stay here in Plum Creek, America, to help. I stay for baby. And," she finished, her voice trembling, "for me."

Try as he might, Jonathan could think of nothing to say. God in heaven, he was cursed. Tess was dead, leaving an infant he couldn't bear to touch or even look at because it reminded him so much of her. Mayor Brumbaugh was stumbling blindly toward disaster; and now Cyrus Peck would descend on him with another tirade about his "bad leg." This time he'd give the crotchety old farmer some fifty-dollar advice: Work an hour a day and mind his own business!

On top of this, he had Miss Erika Scharf to contend with. A more determined, maddening young woman he had never encountered. What god had he offended that such furies pursued him?

More to the point, what should he do about them? About *her.*

He contemplated the crown of honey-colored braids wound on top of her head. He would be civil, he decided. He would swallow his anger and accept the goat. It was a good-hearted deed, after all. And she was right about the milk.

He would overlook the incident this time. Let her stay. But one more disaster—just one more unsettling event in his already unraveling world—and that would be that.

Baby or no baby, he would send Erika Scharf on her way.

Chapter Five

Erika watched the doctor tramp onto the back porch and stalk through the kitchen door. The screened panel swung shut behind him with a resounding *thwap.*

She knew she had overstepped. She had "taken too much upon herself," Mrs. Benbow had warned when Erika appeared with the goat. Worse than disturbing the housekeeper, she had angered Dr. Callender, made him so furious his eyes burned like smoldering coals when he spoke to her.

Surely he knew she meant no harm to him, or to his flowers? His wife's flowers, she amended. Why could he not see that zinnias were not as important as milk for his child?

Unless... Erika paused at the top porch step. Unless the child did not matter to him. Thoughtful, she moved into the kitchen and approached the ramrod-straight figure of Adeline Benbow, swishing an over-size iron spoon back and forth in the stockpot.

"Excuse, please, Mrs. Benbow."

"Overstepped, ye did, traipsing out to bargain on your own," the housekeeper snapped. "Told you so this morning. Got no more sense than a butterfly." She banged the spoon against the side of the pot for emphasis.

"*Ja,*" Erika said in a low voice.

"Use English, girl! You will never learn, other-wise."

"Yes," Erika repeated. "You are correct."

"And just who's going to milk that animal, I ask you?" the housekeeper demanded.

"I will. And feed it, too. Papa had a goat back in old country."

"Hmmph. It's just too much for the doctor after all that's happened," the housekeeper huffed. "Los-ing Miss Tess when they'd just begun their life to-gether...well, it knocked him plumb sideways. Days he'd spend just staring at the bed where she had lain during her torment. Nights, too, staring and staring and seeing nothing. I'm surprised he drove the buggy to town today. Hasn't set foot outside these walls since the funeral three weeks ago."

"Maybe he visit the grave?" Erika ventured.

Mrs. Benbow shot her an odd look. "Maybe." The corners of her thin mouth turned down, and her stirring arm slowed to a stop. An unfocused look came into her eyes.

Erika seized her chance. "What was lady like?"

"Miss Tess?" The stirring resumed, rhythmic figure eights accompanying her words. "Miss Tess was... Her people were from Savannah. Well-to-do they were, before the war. Miss Tess, she had most everything she ever wanted, and that included the doctor. One day he came to call on her father, Colonel Rowell, and the next day he and Miss Tess were engaged."

"Why did doctor go to that place, Savannah?"

"Colonel Rowell was a surgeon during the war. He found a new way to set broken bones, and—"

"And doctor want to learn?" Erika finished for her.

"Saints, no! Doctor knows all about such things from his training in Scotland, you see. He went to Savannah to thank Colonel Rowell for saving his own father's life after the battle of Shiloh."

"And he meet Miss Tess and marry her? She was very beautiful?"

"Oh my, yes," the housekeeper murmured. "Hair like black silk, she had. And eyes so green they looked like emeralds."

"And?" Erika prompted. An insatiable curiosity about the woman who had been mistress of this fine house, and the doctor's affection for her, gnawed at

her insides. She wanted to know all about the woman
Dr. Callender had loved so much his child—even his
own life—seemed unimportant now that she was
gone.

"Well," the housekeeper continued, "Miss Tess
was cultured in the Southern way. She had a lovely
voice, and she accompanied herself on the harp. She
had fine taste in gowns, too—always wore the latest
styles from Paris."

Erika glanced down at her plain blue denim work
skirt and the toes of her sensible shoes peeking from
beneath the hem. She could never be a lady because
her feet were too big and her tastes too simple. She
was a working girl through and through, a poor shoe-
maker's daughter with rough English speech and un-
tutored manners. Such things could be learned, she
supposed. But even if one had a quick mind, it required generations of breeding and practice in manners to make a real lady.

The housekeeper sighed and slid the lid onto the
simmering soup kettle. "But for all that, Miss Tess
didn't—" She broke off and turned toward the sink.

Erika pricked up her ears. But? Miss Tess didn't
what? "Yes?" she invited.

She wanted to know about Mrs. Callender as a
person. What kind of woman planted brilliant scarlet
flowers in a thin, straight line like carefully spaced
soldiers marching toward the front steps? Had Mrs.

Callender been a kind woman? Did she like to laugh? Was she warm and caring as well as beautiful?

"Miss Tess never cared much for... Ah, well, never you mind. The bairn's beginnin' to wail, do ye hear? You'd best warm that milk you set such store by. I put your bucket in the pantry cooler. After that, you can help me with the ironing. I got too much starch in the doctor's shirts again, and they scorch easy."

Tess never cared for what? Erika wanted to shout, but Mrs. Benbow dismissed her with a wave. She pondered the unanswered question all the way up the stairs to the nursery. Perhaps later. She would spend all afternoon in the sweltering kitchen, helping the housekeeper with the ironing. Maybe then the old woman would finish that intriguing sentence.

But she did not. Erika labored for hours over the starched white shirts as the baby slept in the nursery upstairs. By late afternoon her hands ached from lifting the heavy, nickel-plated sadiron and guiding it over the pleated shirtfronts. The six-mile walk out to Cyrus Peck's farm and back early this morning hadn't bothered Erika's strong legs a bit, but pushing the heavy iron back and forth over acres of white linen made her shoulders ache.

The housekeeper smoothed sheets and pillowcases with a second iron until she plopped exhausted into

the single chair next to the stove. "Teatime," she
announced in her raspy voice.

The thought of drinking a cup of scalding tea made
Erika groan out loud. The kitchen was stifling, the
air hot and heavy with moisture, the smell of scorch
and tomato puree suffocating. She longed for a cool
drink of spring water.

"You have a complaint, missy?" Mrs. Benbow
queried, an unpleasant edge to her voice.

"*Nein*. No. Is very hot. I warm easy."

The housekeeper sniffed. "A hothouse girl. But
you work hard, I'll say that for ye."

"Papa used to say I do everything 'hard.' I do not
like halfway things."

Mrs. Benbow glanced up. "Your father is dead?"

Erika nodded. "Mama, too. Of fever, last year. We
do not have doctor in my village."

A curious look crossed the housekeeper's face.
"You mean you came to America alone? All by
yourself?"

"*Ja*. No other way. No one in village want to
leave, even though things there very bad. So I come
alone."

"Were...weren't you frightened?"

"Oh, yes. I come anyway. Nobody see how I
shake on inside."

The housekeeper rose and set the teakettle on the
stove. "I came with my Donald. I didna want to

leave my home, but Donald wanted to build ships in America. Men are like that. They want to *do* things.''

"I also want," Erika replied. "I want to speak good American, and be able to write, so I can become citizen. Maybe someday vote."

"Vote! My stars, girl, are ye daft?"

Erika fished in her apron pocket for her notebook. "How spell 'daft,' please?"

"Never you mind. All a woman ought to want is a husband and babes of her own. All I wanted was my Donald, but he up and died in Philadelphia three years after we were married. I have been with the Callender family ever since."

The kettle began to sing. Erika lifted it off the hot stove and poured the steaming water into a flowered china teapot. "I am sad you lose husband," she said in a soft voice. "But glad you are here in Plum Creek."

Mrs. Benbow jerked upright. "Are you, now? Then it's daft you are for sure! I haven't been—" She broke off. "Why in the world are ye glad?"

Erika handed the older woman a mug of tea. "Because," she said slowly, "you learn—I mean, teach me things."

"I do? You've been here just three days, missy! Just what is it I've taught you?"

Erika cradled the warm mug of tea in her hands. "You do not like me, but you care for doctor. I learn is possible to 'get along.' And I watch at dinner. You show me what spoon to eat soup with, which glass for water.''

She purposely avoided mentioning how she learned the difference between the blue flowered vegetable dish and the ceramic washbowl she now used for bathing the baby.

Mrs. Benbow gaped at her, her snapping black eyes widening as she peered over the rim of her mug.

''And I learn also about doctor's wife,'' Erika continued.

''Miss Tess? Now, why on earth…'' The older woman's voice trailed away.

''Tomorrow I replace flowers. Want to do what is proper, like real lady would.''

The housekeeper's thin gray eyebrows went straight up. ''If you don't mind some advice, child, I'd leave well enough alone about those flowers. You've done enough for one week.''

She plunked her mug down on the table and rose. ''Now, let's just finish up these few pieces of linen before I have to start supper.''

A fluttery Tithonia Brumbaugh swept open the front door of the mayor's two-story house on Chestnut Street. ''Why, good afternoon, Dr. Callender,'' she warbled. ''I didn't expect a call so soon after—''

Jonathan cut the plump woman off with a curt nod.

The mayor's wife had an unerring knack for saying the wrong thing at the wrong time. "Is the mayor in?" he inquired, his tone brusque.

"Why, no. Plotinus is over at the bank, where he spends most Tuesdays. Won't you come in?" She peered at his face. "Forgive me, Jonathan, but you look dreadful. Is anything wrong?"

Jonathan ground his teeth. *Everything* was wrong.

"Thank you, no. I'll drop in at the bank." He tipped his hat and retreated to the buggy. Daisy jerked forward before the whip snapped over her head.

So he looked "dreadful," did he? And he'd forgotten again what day of the week it was. At this rate, he would never regain his equilibrium.

Damn Tess, anyway. It had been an uphill struggle ever since the day he laid eyes on her, all ruffles and furbelows, in Colonel Rowell's Savannah drawing room. She'd torn up his heart and tossed it away as casually as she poured tea and ordered the servants about.

When he reached Main Street, he slowed the mare to a walk. By the time he stopped the buggy in front of the bank, Jonathan had calmed himself and tried to forgive Tess for the hundredth time for setting her cap for him and then dying.

"Summon Mr. Brumbaugh," he ordered the

young man behind the wire cage. "Tell him it's urgent."

"Yessir, Dr. Callender, right away. Say, Ma's sure been feelin' better since you gave her those pills last month. What's in 'em, anyway?"

"Carbohydroxygenate," Jonathan said shortly. They were plain sugar pills, but he didn't think it any of the boy's business. What Mrs. Ellis needed was attention, not medication.

"Mr. Brumbaugh?" he reminded.

The youth ducked his head and disappeared through an inner doorway. In a moment he was back, gesturing Jonathan forward through the swinging wrought-iron gate.

"Go right on in, Doc. The mayor's been expecting you."

"I'll just bet he has," Jonathan muttered under his breath. Four long strides and he entered the bank president's inner sanctum.

The round, florid-faced man rose from behind the spotless desk. "Jonathan, good to see you." He extended a beefy, freckled hand.

"Plotinus, let's not play games. You know you dislike the sight of me. You'll like it even less when you know what I came to say."

"Now look, Jon, can't we agree to—"

"We cannot," Jonathan snapped. "Or rather, I cannot," he said, softening his tone. "Dammit, man, you've got to swing the vote on a new water system. I've walked every mile of Plum Creek these past few weeks. We've got privy and barnyard waste seeping into the water along a ten-mile stretch north of town. Drinking water pumped from that creek is contaminated.''

"Yes, yes. You've said it all before, Jon. We're getting tired of hearing—"

"It's dangerous, 'Tinus. Polluted water brings disease.''

"Aw, come on now, Jon. You're expectin' a disaster like you read about in those back East newspapers you're always quotin'. But hell, my house and your house get their water from wells, so we have nothing to worry about.''

Jonathan grabbed the mayor's shirtfront and pulled him up nose-to-nose. "Plotinus, you simpleminded ass, don't you realize that, wells or no wells, if we have cholera here, the whole town will suffer? You, me, everybody?''

Sweat stood out on the mayor's mottled face. "Just how come you're so sure?''

"Because I'm a physician," Jonathan snapped. "Because I've seen the bacterium under a microscope!''

"Dr. Chilcoate says—"

"Good God, man, Chilcoate's not a qualified doctor! He's a medicine hawker, not a physician. Come on, 'Tinus, I need a vote.'' He released the perspiring man, steadied him with one hand while the shorter man regained his balance.

"We need the water system," he continued in a milder tone. "You know we do."

"Mebbe. But there's no more I can do, I'm afraid. Council already decided the matter. Nothing more can be accomplished, this year at any rate." The mayor straightened his shirt collar with shaking hands. "You oughtta go away for a rest, Jon. Been strung up kinda tight since—"

"You know, and I know," Jonathan said between gritted teeth, "that this has nothing to do with Tess's..." He couldn't say the word.

"Sure, Jon, I know. You're just doin' your job." He reached up, clapped a thick hand on Jonathan's shoulder. "Now get out of my office and let me do mine."

"You're a damn fool, 'Tinus," Jonathan snapped.

"I know. Always have been, I guess. Leastways I've got no power over the council members to force another vote."

Jonathan clamped his jaw shut in frustration. He couldn't just give up. He didn't know what else to do, but he had to think of something. The health of an entire town was at stake.

"I want you to try, anyway. Call another meeting."

The mayor worked his lower lip. "I'll try. But don't hold your breath. And stay away this time. You're gettin' folks riled up with all your talk about horse dung and bugs."

Numb with disbelief, Jonathan drove back to Maple Street and the house he had shared with Tess. Somehow, now that his wife was gone, his whole life shattered, it was important—desperately important—that he try to save Plum Creek.

A sickening feeling of failure rose inside him. Now that the baby was ensconced upstairs, out of his study, he could once again pore over his medical journals from the East and abroad. Much good it did him.

With foreboding, he noted that the leaves of trees that had been frothy with blossoms in May were even now brown and sere around the edges. Midday temperatures had hovered around the hundred-degree mark for over a month, and the thick pall of road dust swirling about Daisy's feet smelled dry and smoky. The worst heat of this long summer was still ahead.

But there might still be time to find a suitable building—a barn, a warehouse, even a church cellar—to scrub down for use as a temporary hospital if the need arose. He thought of Tess, and the familiar knot of anger tightened around him like a hangman's noose. *She didn't die on purpose,* he reminded himself. But he still felt abandoned. It felt like pure, unadulterated hell.

He stopped the buggy, laid the reins on the bench and climbed out. "The irony, old girl," he said to the mare as he unhitched her and led her toward the barn, "is that I finally have all the time I need for my medical practice. But now there's no joy in it."

It was all wrong. Tess had always wanted more of him than he could give. She'd resented his commitment to medicine, the long days spent seeing patients, the emergencies that called him out in the dead of night. To be honest, he had chafed under her misguided nagging.

He had fallen in love with her that day in Savannah, deeply in love. But in the short time they'd had together, they couldn't seem to balance passion and resentment. He regretted that he hadn't been able to manage things differently—make Tess happy as his wife.

And now it was over. His time with her was past.

Is life always like that? he wondered. *Always learning too late what went wrong?*

Chapter Six

Jonathan rounded the corner of the barn and started across the lawn toward the front porch. What an ass he'd been in Plotinus Brumbaugh's office this morning. He'd lost his sense of perspective and his temper, as well. He wouldn't be surprised if the mayor put it out that Jonathan was deranged.

Right now, he needed to be alone. He'd hole up in his study, a stiff whiskey at his elbow, and get a grip on himself. As close as he was to the edge, he didn't want to blunder into Mrs. Benbow or that slip of a German girl. She already regarded him as an ogre. He'd seen it in her eyes that first day—a wary, assessing look, as if she expected him to bite.

Mrs. Benbow would tut-tut when she discovered the empty whiskey glass and the telltale smell of spirits, but he didn't care a whit. He was accountable to no one. His sanity outweighed the disapproval of his housekeeper, even one who'd been with his family as long as Mrs. Benbow had. This was *his* home, his sanctuary. The world outside seemed unreliable. Treacherous.

For the first time in his life, he acknowledged, he could not control events by force of will. But he'd be damned if he'd change one thing about the few things he *could* govern—and one of them was his residence and another was his private study.

Tess had come into his life and been taken from him, and there had been nothing he could do about it. His sense of self, his trust in those things he had valued—knowledge, love, even his skill as a physician—had been shaken to the core. He needed... what? Privacy? Escape?

He needed sameness, he knew that much. Something on which to anchor his equilibrium.

He skirted the expanse of green grass, inhaling the comforting, earthy smells of summer: honeysuckle, the peppery hint of horse manure, wood smoke. Cicadas screamed in the plum tree.

Four steps from the front walkway he brought himself up short. "What the devil?" He raked an unsteady hand through his hair.

A new crop of scarlet zinnias poked their bright heads up along the square cement stepping stones Tess had insisted on. But instead of bordering the path in the neat, orderly line he was used to seeing, the new plants were arranged in masses, mingled with clumps of purple woods iris and drifts of sky-blue pincushion flowers. It looked like a riotous dance of blooms casually swirling in the general direction of the front steps.

He sucked in a breath. Never in a month of Sundays would Tess have tolerated such a wild-looking garden!

"Good God almighty! Who did this?"

Something clanked onto the cement, and Jonathan jerked his head up. Beside the steps leading up to the veranda, a blue-clad figure crouched over the garden bed. Slowly she rose to face him, propping dirt-smudged hands on her hips.

"*I* did this."

The words came from under a floppy-brimmed blue straw hat.

Jonathan's gaze moved from Erika to the flower bed behind her where more zinnias, violet iris and rose-red valerian rubbed shoulders in an untamed jungle of blooms. It was a horticultural kaleidoscope of shapes and colors. Jonathan hated it.

"This," he said testily, "is not what Tess would have done."

"No, is not. Is what *I* have done."

Jonathan eyed the wooden flat of valerian plants at her feet, the wild iris spilling out the top of the bulging gunnysack. "What in God's name gave you the idea you could just waltz out here and—"

"Mr. Zabersky," she interrupted. "Next door

neighbor. Is good gardener. He helps me get plants, but I decide where to put.''

"And what, may I ask, did you bargain away this time?'' Jonathan braced himself to hear that Theodore Zabersky, a man who had never been sick a day in his life, would now expect a free consultation for some nonexistent affliction.

Erika raised her chin, her blue eyes flashing with indignation. ''I did not bargain,'' she said. ''I pay for.''

"All of this?'' He gestured at the half-empty flat.

"The curly petals came from the woods. Mr. Zabersky digs them for me.''

"Curly petals? The iris, you mean.''

"*Ja.* Iris. I not know how to say.'' She bent to retrieve her trowel from the walkway. ''Almost finished. Then I will feed baby and have tea.''

Jonathan groaned aloud. He, too, was ''almost finished.'' But he would have whiskey, not tea. A double shot, and the sooner the better. *Oh, God, what would Tess...*

In the next moment he felt a hiccuping sob rise from his belly. He clamped down on it, hard, suppressing it through sheer willpower. He stared down at the traitorous array of flowers planted in Tess's front garden bed. Suddenly he felt as if he were viewing the scene from a great distance through a sepia-toned lens.

Tess would never see this. She was no longer here. She would never again set foot on the earth. *Never.*

His jaw clenched. Tears stung into his eyes, and from the depths of his soul he cried out in silent anguish. *Why, God? Why?*

He covered his face with his hands and turned away.

Stunned, Erika stared at him. She had intended to please him with her morning's work; instead, she now realized she had done something terribly wrong. Her heart ached over the hurt she had unknowingly caused.

The doctor kept his back to her, but a muffled choking noise told her he was weeping. The sound ripped into her belly. Papa had wept like that when Mama died. She had felt the same gut-wrenching anguish, the same helplessness, then as she did now.

She dropped the trowel and moved toward him. Laying her hand on his sleeve, she tugged him a quarter turn toward her and wrapped her arms about his shuddering frame.

"Cry," she whispered. "Is good to let out."

With a stifled moan he pulled her tight, pressed his face against her shoulder. His entire body trembled.

Erika held him, smoothing the dark curls from his forehead, crooning the words of a German lullaby. He smelled of dust and shaving soap. Her heart skipped, faltered, and then hurtled on.

Gradually he quieted. At last he lifted his head and looked at her with weary gray eyes. Their gazes locked, and in that instant Erika felt a curious warmth envelop her, as if the earth had stopped turning and the sun shed all its light on this one spot.

Shaken, she stepped away from him. She had no right.

"I feed baby now," she managed. "Finish garden later." She turned to leave, a nameless bird beating its wings against her breastbone.

He reached out one hand and stopped her. "I apologize, Miss Scharf. I don't know what came over me."

"I know," she replied quietly. "Is grief. After, you will be better."

She moved away from him, afraid he would see her face, read her feelings. When she reached the veranda, she heard his voice behind her.

"I will reimburse you for the plants."

Without answering, Erika closed the front door behind her and stood perfectly still. Some things in life were beyond price. No amount of money could pay for what he had taken from her in the few seconds she had stood clasped in his arms.

She closed her eyes and clenched her hands into fists. Her heart was worth more than all the flowers in the universe.

Gwendolyn's..."

...

Chapter Seven

Tithonia Brumbaugh stabbed her needle into the
Sawtooth Star quilt stretched on top of her broad
dining-room table. "Ladies, this is scandalous!" She
tugged the backing material toward her.

"Oh, don't be so dramatic," Jane Munrow re-
monstrated in her usual raspy tone. She jerked
the quilt to realign it. "It's not scandalous. It's
merely...unusual."

Gwendolyn Shaunessey propped both her thin
arms on the table. "Unusual! Oh, come, Jane. A
young girl alone in that house with the doctor? Of
course it's scandalous!"

The three other women gathered around Tithonia's
polished walnut table squirmed on their horsehair
chairs.

"Maybe not scandalous," Mary Zabersky interjected into the silence, "but Tithonia's right. It is

definitely improper.'' She ducked her head, concentrating on making tiny, even stitches around a square of lilac gingham. Her dark curls fell forward to obscure her face.

"Precisely," Gwendolyn breathed. "Im-proper." She accented the first syllable.

"Well, I think you're all being too catty about something we know nothing about.'' Susan Ransom's voice rose, as it always did when she was piqued. As the newest and youngest member of the group, Susan was the most outspoken of the women. Also, she was unmarried, which placed her squarely at the bottom of the pecking order.

"*You* know nothing about it," Gwendolyn pointed out. "That is not to say that *we* know nothing. *We* know quite a bit. At least, Tithonia does."

Tithonia wove her needle into her half-finished square of blue-checked gingham and rose. "Ladies, it's time for our tea."

A scandal was a scandal, and the banker's wife loved nothing better than laying out the delectable details before the five-member Presbyterian Ladies Quilting Circle, along with her vanilla sugar cookies and thick slices of Swedish apple cake.

The other ladies carefully rolled up the quilt and pushed back their chairs. Tithonia poured and handed out steaming cups while the plates of cookies and cake slices were passed hand to hand. Mary clattered her cup onto the saucer. "Have you seen her? She's very unusual looking. Wears her hair in braids around her head, like a crown. And eyes like morning glories."

"She's from Germany," Jane said shortly. Her clipped tone betrayed her disdain for the direction of the conversation.

"I heard she is an orphan. Hasn't a penny to her name."

"How old is she?"

"Can she read and write?"

"What wages does he pay her, do you think?"

"Such a shame what she did to Tess's zinnia border! Imagine, mixing purple iris with valerian!"

"Maybe she's color blind!"

The ladies chattered like busy hens until Susan Ransom suddenly set down her china saucer with a thunk. "Really, ladies! I think this Erika person is taking entirely too much of our time and attention. After all, we are here to quilt, are we not?"

Silence dropped over the company for almost a full minute. Finally Mary Zabersky cleared her throat and mopped a delicate embroidered handerchief over her upper lip. "What does Mrs. Benbow say about her?"

"Mrs. Benbow," answered Jane, brushing cake crumbs from her ample bosom, "doesn't say anything about anything, much less about Erika Scharf."

Gwendolyn's blue eyes widened. "Nothing at all?"

"Nothing."

"But she's Dr. Callender's housekeeper! She's lived there for years, even before Tess, I mean, the late Mrs. Callender—even before he brought his wife to Plum Creek. She must know something!"

Tithonia stared at her friend. Widowed four years before as the result of a logging accident, Gwendolyn had herself nursed hopes of attracting the handsome physician. Her disappointment when he had brought Tess home after his trip to Savannah had festered into quiet despair.

Tithonia rose to refill Gwendolyn's cup, then circled the table with the dish of lemon slices. "Of course Mrs. Benbow knows things."

"What things?" Mary's dark eyes snapped in anticipation.

"Yes, what? Tell us, Tithonia. Don't keep us on pins and needles!"

"Well," the banker's wife began, relishing her role as the purveyor of community intelligence.

"Yes?"

"What did she say?"

"Hush!" Gwendolyn hissed. "Let Tithonia speak."

Tithonia settled herself into the upholstered chair at the head of the table. "Now, Adeline Benbow isn't one to gossip, mind you. It isn't so much what she says as what she doesn't say." She glanced about at the ladies of her quilting circle. "Adeline attends services each Sunday, as you know. Erika Scharf does not."

"You mean she's a Catholic?"

"I mean, she does not attend church. Period."

Jane sniffed. "And what does that prove? One's religion is a private matter."

"But my dear Jane, don't you see?"

"See what? The cream, please, Mary. See what?" Jane repeated.

"Why, they're alone in that house, of course. For an entire morning." She paused dramatically. "Every Sunday."

Jane shrugged and half-filled her cup from the cream pitcher as it came her way. "So?"

Tithonia lowered her voice to a whisper. *"Together."*

"Well, of course, together. It's the doctor's house. He lives there."

Jane's scratchy tone set Tithonia's teeth on edge. "And *she* lives there, too!" Tithonia added tea to the milky contents of Jane's cup.

"So does Mrs. Benbow," Jane snapped. "Where else would the doctor's household help live?"

"That is not the point, Jane," Tithonia retorted. "The point is— Oh, Mary, do have a second piece of cake. You look a bit peaked. The point is, they are not chaperoned.''

''Chaperoned!'' Susan's cup again clattered onto her saucer. ''Since when do servants and their employer need a—''

''Since Eve tempted Adam with that apple, my dear.'' Tithonia's chest swelled in indignation. ''You are young, yet, Miss Ransom. And have much to learn, I see.''

''Mrs. Benbow had lived alone in that house with Dr. Callender—alone, I repeat—for at least ten years until Tess arrived,'' Jane protested.

''Mrs. Benbow is in her sixties. Erika Scharf is only twenty-five.''

''Twenty-four,'' Mary corrected. ''At least, that's what my father says. He helped her plant that awful jumble of flowers in the front garden. He even built a shed for that dreadful goat!''

''Twenty-five, twenty-four. What difference does it make?'' Tithonia snapped. ''I recognize my duty as a Christian woman.''

Nothing was going to hinder her righteous cause. She'd made up her mind, and no one, certainly not her quilting circle ladies, was going to change it. She'd hoped to enlist them as allies, but some of them—particularly Jane and young Susan Ransom—were addlepated beyond belief.

She'd set things right the very first thing in the morning.

"Ladies, more tea?"

Adeline Benbow laid the last gold-rimmed breakfast plate on the stack in the cabinet and hung the damp cotton dish towel beside the stove to dry. Already the morning air was hot, and the fire she'd built in the firebox added to the heat in her kitchen. When the insistent knocking at the back door started, Adeline mopped her face and neck with a limp lace handerchief and smoothed her skirt for company.

"Adeline?" Tithonia Brumbaugh's piercing voice came through the door.

"A bit early for a social call, isn't it, Tithonia?" Adeline said, opening the door. "I've barely finished washing up the breakfast things."

"Forget the breakfast things. This is more important."

Adeline narrowed her eyes. "Now, what could be more important than a clean kitchen?"

Tithonia's bosom expanded, puffing up her plump torso until the waterfall fichu on the rose sateen morning dress trembled. Adeline thought she resembled a smug, worm-stuffed robin.

"Out with it, Tithonia. I've got work to do."

"Well, then," Tithonia breathed in a conspiratorial tone. "Have you not considered what people will think? What they are saying?"

"Saying about what? Tithonia, I declare, you can be oblique at times."

The mayor's wife blinked. "May I sit down, my dear? My bunions, you know." She settled onto a hard-backed chair and crossed one ankle over the other. Her black leather shoes barely touched the shiny painted floor. "Oblique, is it?" Her flushed forehead creased into a frown.

Adeline suppressed a smile. Tithonia's vocabulary was limited to the words in *Godey's Lady's Book* and the Presbyterian hymnal.

"Oblique," Adeline reiterated. "Come to the point, Tithonia. I haven't got all day."

"Well," Tithonia replied, lowering her voice. "We understand there is a young woman living here. A Miss Scharf?"

Adeline reached behind her to retie her loose apron. "We? Who is 'we'?"

"My quilting circle ladies."

The housekeeper nodded. Just as she thought. What Plum Creek gossip didn't originate around Tithonia's quilting table was certainly embellished there. And Tithonia did most of the embellishing.

"Therefore, my dear," Tithonia continued, "we want to express our concern about—"

The Dutch doors separating the kitchen from the

dining room swung open, and Erika flew in. "Mrs. Benbow, I have just to warm the baby's—oh, please excuse. I did not know was company here."

"Erika, this is Tithonia Brumbaugh, the mayor's wife."

Erika curtsied. "Am honored, missus."

"Miss Scharf is the baby's nurse," the housekeeper added. "Tess—Mrs. Callender—engaged her before she passed away."

Adeline watched Tithonia's sharp eyes take in Erika's simple blue chambray work skirt and crisp white blouse. Her gazed moved from the crown of honey-colored braids adorning the younger woman's head to her nipped-in waist to her sensible laced canvas shoes. She felt a hum of energy in her chest when Tithonia frowned.

"Why, you're a mere child, my dear! It's fortunate that I came before it's too late."

Erika's hands stilled on the ties of her apron. "I am twenty and four, Missus Mayor. Not a child."

Tithonia's eyes widened. "All the more reason for me to speak out."

Adeline waited. Tithonia wasn't used to being put on the defensive. The housekeeper knew Erika well enough to deduce it would only be a matter of time before the inevitable happened.

Erika's blue eyes snapped. "I am glad you speak out. Will be more for me to learn." She patted her apron pocket where Adeline knew she kept her English notebook.

Tithonia swallowed. "Good. Having an open mind will make my mission easier."

"Yes, missus." Erika withdrew her notebook and fished in her pocket for a pencil. Adeline yanked the shopping-list pencil off its string. Without a word she handed it to Erika.

Tithonia straightened her shoulders. "It has come to our attention, Miss Scharf, that you are residing in Dr. Callender's house."

"Oh, *ja.* Yes," Erika replied. "Is so beautiful and big, with windows everywhere! I am happy to be re-siding here. And baby is happy, too."

"But do you think it is proper?"

Erika blinked. "Proper? Oh, yes. I learn quickly about baby." She flashed Adeline a smile. "Is proper."

"But you *live* here."

"*Ja.* I do."

"With…uh…Dr. Callender."

"*Ja.* Beautiful house belongs to him." Erika turned puzzled eyes on the mayor's wife.

"I live here, too, Tithonia," Adeline reminded her. "In fact, I've lived here with Dr. Callender for the past twelve years. Just—" she took care to enunciate each word "—the doctor and myself."

"Oh, Adeline, *you* don't matter!"

The housekeeper's chin came up. "And why not?"

"Adeline, for heaven's sake. You're the housekeeper, that's why!"

Erika opened her notebook. "Why does not housekeeper matter?"

"Because…because… Oh, Adeline, you see, don't you? You're…ah…old, and she—Miss Scharf—is young. Eligible. It's a matter of propriety."

Erika scribbled in her notebook. Then she raised her head and met Tithonia Brumbaugh's gaze. "I do not see difference between Mrs. Benbow and myself. We live here in house. We work for doctor. I work upstairs, take care of baby. Mrs. Benbow work downstairs, take care of house and cooking. Oh, I forget—I care for goat, too."

"Goat!"

"Oh, *ja*." Erika's smile made her eyes sparkle. "For milk."

"The babe was colicky," Adeline explained. "The doctor recommended goat's milk, and Erika—"

"Yes, yes, I see." Tithonia squirmed on the hard chair.

"And I plant flowers along walk—pretty ones, from woods, to make beautiful again."

"So I noticed," Tithonia observed dryly.

An awkward silence fell. Adeline waited, unconsciously holding her breath, as Erika laid the pencil down on the baking table and faced the mayor's wife.

"So, I do wrong thing?"

"Well..." Tithonia hesitated. "Well, no. Not exactly."

Adeline opened her mouth to voice the question that had been nagging at her, then thought better of it. She pressed her lips together. Mayor's wife or not, Tithonia Brumbaugh was not going to be allowed to judge the workings of Adeline's bailiwick. For twelve years she'd managed the smoothest running household in Plum Creek. That and Dr. Callender's comfort were the only things that mattered.

Erika brought the matter to a head with a single innocent question. At least, Adeline assumed it was innocent. But at the moment, the look in the young woman's china-blue eyes was anything but guileless.

"So, Missus Mayor," Erika said slowly, "is wrong what we do?"

"Oh, no, my dear. Not both of you, just...well, you see, you're young and, um, somewhat vulnerable...."

Erika wrote in her notebook. "Vul-ner-a-ble," she murmured. "What mean, please?"

"It means that you—your name, that is—can be damaged."

"And Mrs. Benbow's name not?"

"Mrs. Benbow is a widow. An older woman."

Adeline stiffened but said nothing.

"How can name be damaged, please?"

A brief smile of triumph crossed Tithonia's round face. "Plum Creek is a small but law-abiding community," she said. Her voice, Adeline noted, took on a sanctimonious tone.

"Sharing a house with a member of the opposite sex," the mayor's wife continued, "well, it just isn't done."

"Why is it not?" Erika pursued.

Tithonia gave a nervous hiccup of laughter. "Because people talk about such things. About you. And about the doctor."

"People talk already about me," Erika said. "Mr. Zabersky, man next door, says I am stubborn-headed. Church minister says for me to come on Sundays or will not go to heaven. Grocery keeper says I buy wrong kind of yeast for bread. They are all wrong, except Mr. Zabersky. Is true that I am stubborn-headed."

Adeline added a private word of agreement.

Tithonia's smile faltered. "I mean," she said purposefully, "they will talk about you *and* the doctor. In the same breath."

"Ah, I see now. Doctor makes speeches about dirty water to drink and people get mad. They say he is stubborn-headed, too, that is it?"

Tithonia rolled her eyes in Adeline's direction.

"Yes, you both certainly are stubborn-headed. But that is not quite what I meant. To be blunt, Miss Scharf, your reputation is at stake."

"Because of doctor?"

"Because of you and the doctor, yes."

"Not because of goat, or flower garden nobody likes, or wrong yeast?"

"No."

Erika thought for a moment. Adeline glimpsed a flash of blue fire before the thick lashes flicked down.

"Goat is wrong thing I do. Flowers, too. And maybe yeast. But not doctor. Doctor is not wrong. I am not wrong."

"But—"

"Forgive me, Missus Mayor, but who lives in doctor's house is not your business."

Tithonia gaped at her, her lace-fichued breast swelling in indignation.

All at once Adeline brimmed with energy. She propelled herself into the fray.

"Tithonia, wouldn't you like some of my chamomile tea while we visit? Erika must tend to the babe now. 'Tis past her feeding time."

She settled the teakettle on the stove top and turned to the mayor's wife, who sat staring at the Dutch doors swinging to and fro in Erika's wake.

Well-done, child! You're a canny lass, even if you are a Lutheran!

Chapter Eight

Erika cuddled the small, fragrant body of Marian Elizabeth Callender against her shoulder and paced resolutely up and down the first-floor hallway. "Hush, little one," she crooned. "Hush, now." She traversed the large foyer and made yet another circuit around the front sitting room, turning her body round and round in slow circles in an attempt to calm the crying child.

"So much wailing, little Marian! And so many tears. Come now, can you not smile for me?"

For the past hour she had paced in and out of the downstairs rooms—all but the doctor's study—because it was cooler on the ground floor. Upstairs, the nursery and the other rooms, the sitting room that served as the library, her bedroom, and no doubt the doctor's bedroom, sweltered in the heat radiating from the roof under a relentless August sun. When the baby stopped crying, Erika would tuck her into the portable wicker bassinet she had moved into the front parlor. But would the infant ever cease her wailing?

The child's thin cries continued. Erika sighed. She had cried steadily most of the long, hot afternoon. Erika decided it was the oppressive heat, but not even sponging her with cool water seemed to bring relief. She wasn't wet. No pins poked into the delicate skin. What, then?

Whatever the cause, Erika was tired out. The poor mite herself must be exhausted, she thought. Maybe the baby missed its mama? Erika's heart felt a tiny catch.

The front doorbell shrilled and Erika jerked. All day long, that bell! Since Dr. Callender had resumed seeing his patients, a constant stream of townspeople trailed in and out from morning until past teatime. Half the residents of Plum Creek seemed to be ailing.

She reached for the polished brass doorknob. "Why, Mr. Zabersky! What I do for you?"

The tall, bearded man on the veranda removed his hat and smiled at Erika. "You, my child, can do nothing." He raised his voice to be heard over the baby's wailing. "Dr. Callender, a little something, perhaps."

"Ah, you have engagement—no, is wrong word. Appointment, I mean?"

"Yes," the older man affirmed. His bushy silver mustache twitched, and his eyebrows rode up and down.

Erika jiggled the baby at her shoulder and patted the tiny back.

"May I come in?" Mr. Zabersky said.

Erika's face heated. "Oh, forgive, please! All day baby cry and I am pre...pre..."

"Preoccupied?" He shut the door quietly behind him.

"*Ja.* Pre-occupy. Come in, please, Mr. Zabersky. I will tell doctor you are here."

She rapped on the closed door to the second parlor, which served as the physician's office. A small room behind it—a maid's room at one time—was used as an examining room.

"Enter," a resonant male voice called.

Erika pushed the door open. The doctor raised his head from the stack of blue medical files on his desk. "Yes?" A subtle edge sharpened the tone of his voice.

"Mr. Zabersky is here to see you," she ventured. Why did he always snap at her so? He was like a caged lion, and his temper, so short! Maybe that, too, was because of the relentless summer heat.

"Ah, yes," he said. "Ask Mrs. Benbow to bring us some tea, would you? I missed lunch again."

The doctor had worked through both breakfast and

lunch, Erika noted in silence. Until an hour ago, patients had filled every chair in the spacious front hall.

"Ted? Come right in." Jonathan rose from his desk, extending his hand to the older man. "More headaches, is that it? I thought we had them licked this time. But I've a new idea to try...."

The rest was inaudible as the physician's resonant voice faded behind the closing door.

And then suddenly the door cracked open, and the lion roared. "Stop that child's caterwauling, Miss Scharf! It's giving *me* a headache!"

Erika turned away. *That child?* Not "Marian Elizabeth," or even "my daughter"? What kind of father was he? What kind of man?

Insensitive, a voice within her spoke. *Incomprehensible. Irascible.* Just yesterday she'd used the dictionary to make a list of new English words to describe Dr. Jonathan Callender. *Illogical* and *ill-mannered,* she added mentally. She conveniently forgot her very last entry. *Intriguing.*

Tonight, she resolved, she'd start on the *J* words. She felt better already. Heartened, she moved toward the kitchen, rocking the baby gently up and down. "Please, please, dear baby, stop crying. Your papa it makes angry, and your mama up in heaven will not be happy."

She spoke briefly to Mrs. Benbow, just emerging from the pantry with a large towel-draped bowl of rising bread dough in her hands. Then she half walked, half danced her way into the sitting room.

"Ssh, ssh, *Liebchen*." She spun this way and that, avoiding the long rocker runners, the polished walnut harp in the corner, the heavy end table covered with a lacy black shawl. Around and around she waltzed, softly humming an old tune. Her skirt rippled as she turned.

"*...liegst mir im Herzen...*" she sang. Her hem flared out, brushing against the harp strings with an echoey glissando. Instantly the baby stopped crying.

Erika stared down at the infant, barely able to believe her ears. The reverberation of the harp shimmered in the silence.

Experimentally she plucked a single string with her forefinger, and a lovely note bloomed in the quiet. Marian Elizabeth made a soft cooing noise.

Erika plucked another string, and then another. Even individual notes sounded beautiful, all by themselves, she marveled. Laboriously she picked out the first phrase of a lullaby by ear.

The baby's tiny fist uncurled, and her head settled onto Erika's shoulder. By the end of the second plucked phrase, the child was sound asleep.

Erika tiptoed to the wicker cradle and gently laid her on the smooth white sheet. Still humming, she moved to the harp and stood gazing at it. In the late-afternoon light the wood looked warm, the carved scroll at the top almost fluid. A forest of strings stretched beneath her tentative fingers.

Never before had she heard any sound as heavenly sweet and pure as the notes of a harp. A sharp yearning rose in her, a need so strong it almost frightened her. She wanted to make the instrument sing! Oh, if she could only make more of those beautiful sounds!

"Erika, my dear, would you like to learn?" Mr. Zabersky stood in the doorway.

"What? Oh, I did not see you, Mr. Zabersky."

"Do you wish to play the harp?" The old man's voice was so soft Erika thought she must have dreamed his question.

"I can teach you. I was a musician once."

"Oh, I—I couldn't," Erika demurred. "Harp does not belong to me."

Mr. Zabersky reached a hand into his jacket pocket and withdrew a white paper packet. He shook it. "Pills," he announced with a broad smile. "For my headache. Pay for them later, the doctor says. Maybe I can give you music lessons instead?"

Erika gasped. "Oh, could you? Do you think—do you think doctor would let—that I could really learn?"

"But of course, my child. I am a very fine teacher. I'll come tomorrow, shall I? When the baby sleeps, at…" He withdrew a gold watch from his top trouser pocket and squinted at it. "Four o'clock. Would that be satisfactory?"

Erika opened her mouth to reply and then let it drift shut. Surely she was sound asleep and none of this was really happening! *Satisfactory?* It was superb. Stupendous. Sensational! All the most exciting new many-syllabled words she had learned last week.

"Oh, yes!" Erika breathed. "Oh, thank you. Thank you! I will myself make you some tea after the lesson, so will not interrupt Mrs. Benbow."

Mr. Zabersky made a brief courtly bow. "Until four o'clock, then." He turned to leave, then pivoted back to her. "One small favor, perhaps?"

"Anything," Erika breathed.

"Those delicious buns the housekeeper brought with the tea for Dr. Callender. Do you think possibly…"

"I will make sure to have buns, yes. They are very good. Mrs. Benbow makes them with Demerara sugar and honey."

The old man's black eyes sparkled. "Demerara…and honey," he murmured. "A pleasure."

He retrieved his hat from the oak hat stand in the front hall and stepped to the door. "A most certain pleasure."

Erika felt like laughing and crying all at once. Could it really be that Mr. Zabersky, that kindly old gentleman who had helped her plant wild iris and valerian, was her fairyfolk godmother?

Ah, no, she chided herself. *My mind runs on so, as if I am dreaming. Mr. Zabersky is surely my fairy god*father!

Jonathan raised his eyes from Theodore Zabersky's medical file and stared at the door separating his office from the rest of the house. With one hand he loosened the silk cravat at his neck and ran his forefinger around the inside of his white linen shirt collar. Too much starch again. Ever since Tess—

His throat closed. His housekeeper had lapsed into her own ways since Tess was no longer around to give orders. Mrs. Benbow always added lots of starch to his shirts. It was her stamp of approval in a way.

He prayed Ted Zabersky would be his last patient of the day. After arguing for an hour with Cyrus Peck about his knee joints and trying to convince Mrs. Ellis to boil their water since their place bordered the creek, he had a splitting headache. His temples pounded, and sounds in the heated stillness of late afternoon were intensified until the smallest noise made him wince.

Perhaps he was hallucinating. A moment ago he'd thought he heard Tess's harp. He leaned forward, planted both elbows on his paper-strewn desk and dug his thumbs into his eye sockets. *Tess. Would you have lived if I'd taken you home to Savannah, as you wanted? Or did you despise me so much for making you grow up that you died simply to hurt me?*

"My beautiful, willful Tess," he murmured. "So accomplished at playing the lady, but such a child at heart." She wanted him all to herself every minute of the day. How could he be a husband to her and a physician as well? There simply wasn't enough of him.

He recognized the rage seething below the surface of his grief. Rationally he knew it was better than being numb, as he had been these past terrible weeks, but lately he felt as if his skin were on fire, stung with the brutal points of a thousand needles, like circulation just returning to frozen limbs. Psychosomatic, no doubt. Even so, the painful, almost exquisite sensitivity of the surface of his body persisted day and night.

His mind still felt as if it was asleep, though. Part of him wanted to shake off the torpor crushing him; another part wanted never to wake up from the half-world he'd escaped to. Maybe it would be easier to remain numb.

Odd how the body roused itself, clamored for life, before the spirit was ready. He'd do some research on the phenomenon sometime in the future. If he was to have a future. At times he didn't think so. Other days, like today, he knew he would not. Sensed he would die soon, was perhaps dying even now.

Despite Mrs. Benbow's overstarched collar, his head felt so heavy he could barely hold it upright. If it weren't for the threat of cholera in the town, he would let himself drift off and escape forever.

And what about your baby daughter? He felt a curious blankness where she was concerned. He told himself he felt nothing for her, neither love nor hate. He tried not to think about her. Usually he was successful, but just now, when he thought he'd heard Tess's harp, he found he couldn't keep the child out of his mind.

And Erika Scharf? the insistent voice questioned.

Yes, Erika, too. He tried very hard not to think about the young German girl. Ever since that day when he had clung to the slim woman with the honey-colored hair, he realized he had been avoiding her.

A whisper of sound brushed against his ear. The harp again. *God blast that instrument to kingdom come!* Would he never be free of it? Of Tess?

Into his silent, stifling study drifted four distinct notes, clear and soft as if dropped into his heart from a great height. In an instant he was on his feet, his fists clenched. He strode to the door and jerked it wide.

"Stop it!" His voice boomed inside his head, a

harsh, ugly bellow he'd never imagined he possessed.

An arpeggio faltered, then resumed.

"Stop, I said!" At his shout, the sound ceased.

Before his mind could engage, his legs started forward, propelling him across the hall into the front parlor. He stomped to a halt before the burled walnut instrument.

Erika spun toward him, her hand at her throat. The blue eyes widened at the sight of him, then the bronze lashes swept down.

"What are you doing in here?" he thundered.

She pressed one finger against her lips and gestured toward the tiny form in the wicker cradle. "Come," she whispered.

She moved in front of him, toward the door. The faint scent of lilac emanated from her starched white waist. In spite of himself, Jonathan inhaled sharply.

A wave of longing choked him. Almost of its own volition, his hand reached out to touch her. He caught himself just in time.

Madness. The hunger of his body pushed him into no-man's-land.

"Now," Erika began, her back to him, "you wanted something?" She turned slowly as she finished her sentence.

"Yes," he blurted. "I want... I want..." His brain went blank. Pain sliced through his thoughts.

His body spoke for him. His groin tightened, ached with need. He wanted *her!* There was no mistaking the truth of human physiology. What in God's name was happening to him?

You are beginning to come back to life, the voice inside reminded him.

"Ah, no," he muttered. *I am not ready.*

Some part of you is ready, Jonathan. The healthy part. The normal, male part.

Erika stared at him. "Is something wrong, Doctor?"

"What?"

She jumped at the bark in his voice. "I said—"

"I heard what you said, dammit. No, nothing is wrong."

Everything is wrong. You hunger, but you do not partake.

"You are not telling truth," she said quietly.

Desperately, Jonathan fought to pull himself together. "No, I'm not," he said at last. And then he laughed at the understatement. He was lying, not only to her, but to himself. He knew it. And she knew it.

Tension arced between them, palpable as a hot wind.

"I wish…" Jonathan closed his eyes to shut out the figure before him. He was afraid to trust his tongue, his voice, afraid they would spill words from his mouth he could not condone.

"I wish not to hear the harp," he pronounced with care.

"Very well. I will not disturb—"

"I mean," Jonathan interrupted, his voice rising, "now that Tess... No one is to play it."

"Ah," she breathed. "It reminds you."

Jonathan groaned. It wasn't so much that it reminded him of Tess. Her playing was skilled but cold, somehow. Lifeless. The truth was the sonorous sound of the vibrating strings made him—his body, his soul—ache.

"No, not exactly," he replied. He worked to lower his voice.

Erika regarded him with an open look. "But you do not want—"

The blue of her eyes was so intense it hurt him. After a long, uncomfortable moment, he dropped his gaze.

"Yes," he said quickly. "I do not want anyone, anyone else, to play that harp."

The light went out of her eyes. "But surely, perhaps in time."

"Never." He growled the word.

It was true. He wanted never again to feel the hunger he felt at this moment, to battle the keen, rich awareness of her as a woman and himself as a man.

She clasped her hands together at her waist. Jonathan watched her knuckles whiten as her fingers interlocked. It was a cowardly act, forbidding something only because he feared it. He disliked himself for it. And yet some buried, shadow self took a perverse pleasure in shielding himself, even at her expense. *Good God, how far a man sinks to escape his animal nature.*

Erika remained silent, her expression changing from dumbfounded to merely puzzled. She took a single step backward. "Is wrong thing," she said at last. "You need beautiful things. Music. Sunlight. Things of life."

Jonathan nodded. She was right, of course. She had no idea how much he desired such things, and how terrifying it was. It was frightening to be moved by a lovely sound. The moment had touched his heart, quickened his blood. He was aware that he fought it. With all his strength he resisted coming to life.

To every thing there is a season, Reverend Thomas had intoned at Tess's burial. *A time to love…a time to die.* His time for joy in a woman had passed with Tess's death, and now his heart was sealed tight. He wanted to keep it that way.

Erika squared her shoulders. "Is wrong," she repeated in a low, controlled voice.

Something in her tone gave him pause, as if she

were issuing a subtle challenge. "Not wrong, Miss Scharf," he said wearily. "Merely…" He hesitated. "Unwise."

He could not turn the wheel of seasons. He hadn't the courage.

Erika lifted her chin. "Is wrong," she said again. She stepped past him, moved slowly across the front hall and up the staircase without looking back.

Jonathan inhaled the subtle scent that wafted after her and closed his eyes. The pain in his temples pounded with relentless fury.

Chapter Nine

With trembling hands Erika pulled a damask-covered chair close to the harp and sat down to wait for Mr. Zabersky. Thank goodness Dr. Callender was out for the afternoon! While he was gone, her next-door neighbor would give Erika her first harp lesson. Oh, her insides were so fluttery!

Mrs. Benbow had issued an unbelievable ultimatum during the tea break they had shared in the kitchen yesterday.

"Of course ye must learn to play, my girl! How else will that fitful babe be soothed asleep? And later, it'll help ye get on in this new world."

At the time, Erika wondered what playing a harp had to do with her future success in America, but later, when the sound of young Mary Zabersky's piano playing floated over the lawn separating their adjacent houses, she made the connection.

Making music was a required social art among the ladies of Plum Creek. If she were to belong in America—and she wanted to so much her heart ached!— she must cultivate at least one refined skill. At least, that's what Mrs. Benbow said. Besides, the sweet, ethereal sound of the instrument spoke to her soul, made her spirit sing. When she heard the music made by plucking just a single string, she felt closer to heaven than at any other time in her twenty-four years.

Methodically, Erika prepared for her quiet defiance of Dr. Callender's order. She had dusted the harp and picked a bouquet of indigo iris and purple-red cosmos to arrange in a vase on the side table. Mrs. Benbow had baked a dozen fresh honey-sugar buns and laid them in the warming oven for tea later. Now, as four o'clock drew near, Erika poked at the flowers and confronted her conflicting thoughts.

Dr. Callender would be furious if he discovered what she was doing. But Marian Elizabeth slumbered peacefully in the wicker cradle, and the baby's appetite had perked up since yesterday. Clearly, music was beneficial for the child. That alone would be reason enough to pursue her course of action.

Her hand smoothed the warm burled wood of the harp, tentatively touched the strings. What if she proved to be not gifted in music? What if she simply wasted Mr. Zabersky's valuable time?

After a long moment of pensive thought, she straightened her spine. No matter what, Mr. Zabersky would surely enjoy the pot of tea and Mrs. Benbow's sticky buns. Would it matter so much if she struggled with the instrument and failed?

Oh, yes, it would! She resolved she would not fail. Papa always said if you wanted something enough, God would make it possible. It had happened with Marian Elizabeth. Within Erika's first hour in the spacious Callender home, she had felt the tiny motherless creature capture her heart, wrapping delicate fingers about her sensibilities until she was as besotted as a young girl on midsummer's eve.

And it was happening with Mrs. Benbow. At first the crusty housekeeper could find no good in anything Erika did. According to her, Erika clattered the dishes, neglected to help her polish the silver, lagged at the ironing. But when Erika had begun to share her hopes and dreams about becoming an American, little by little the stiff-backed woman had started to soften.

Mrs. Benbow encouraged Erika to learn not only English conversation but refined table manners and household account keeping. Then just last week, the housekeeper had entrusted her with the grocery shopping at Valey's Mercantile.

And today, here were a dozen sugar buns for Mr. Zabersky!

Oh, she wanted so much to learn how to make music! All she needed was one quiet afternoon each week when Dr. Callender would be out.

At the knock on the front door, Erika's heart leapt. "I will receive!" she called to the housekeeper as she skimmed over the polished oak floor. The *whap-whap* of the Dutch doors between the hall and the kitchen told Erika Mrs. Benbow had retreated.

In the front parlor everything was ready—the harp shiny with polish, the padded chair drawn close, the flowers rearranged for the fourth time as the baby slept.

"Good afternoon, Mr. Zabersky. Please to come in."

The old man removed his hat and clicked his heels in a formal bow. "Well, my dear, are you ready to begin?" He gave her a smile and followed her into the parlor.

The professor showed her how to place her hands on the harp strings, how to strum one note at a time without moving the other fingers or making a buzzing noise. She surprised herself by learning quickly, and she begged for more.

When the hour drew to a close, the gray-bearded music teacher showed Erika two additional exercises to practice during the week. As he demonstrated, he sniffed the air appreciatively.

"Sugar buns," Erika volunteered. "I promise, remember? I will fetch the tea."

Just as she rose from her chair, Mrs. Benbow appeared with a huge silver tray on which teetered her good china teapot, cups and saucers, and a plate heaped with fragrant buns.

Professor Zabersky shot to his feet. Lifting the heavy tray out of the housekeeper's hands, he beamed at her. "This is most kind of you, madam," he said as he settled the tray on the side table.

Mrs. Benbow's eyebrows drew together. "Tea and biscuits is all," she snapped.

"Ah, but what biscuits!" Mr. Zabersky inhaled deeply. "Food for the gods. Ambrosia."

Mrs. Benbow sniffed. But as she swept toward the doorway, her black bombazine skirt swishing at each resolute step, Erika thought the housekeeper's cheeks looked a little pink. Perhaps it was only the heat in the kitchen.

Mr. Zabersky's gaze slowly refocused on Erika as she poured out the tea. "I think you will make a fine musician, Erika."

Erika's hand wobbled. "Oh, do you really think so? How can you already know?"

The old gentleman helped himself to a bun. "Because, my dear, you have the gift." He bit into the honeyed confection. "And I, Theodore Zabersky, have the knowledge. I will give you lessons twice a week.''

''Twice! Oh, but I cannot—''

He held up a cautionary finger. ''If,'' he interjected, ''your Mrs. Benbow will make these heavenly morsels once in a while. That, and your eyes shining as they are now, will be payment enough for a restless old teacher hungry to share music with a kindred soul.''

Tears stung behind Erika's eyelids. Why, the dear old man was lonely! Her heart swelled until it hurt. She wanted music instruction; he wanted company. ''Is fair trade,'' she said.

''Ah, such a businesswoman,'' he teased. ''But you are right. Such hands—'' He lifted her fingers from the teapot handle. ''Perfect for the harp. And such baking...'' He rolled his eyes toward the ceiling. ''Perfect for the harp teacher!''

Perfect, Erika echoed in her mind. She could hardly believe her good fortune. From that fateful day when she'd climbed off the stagecoach and rapped on Dr. Callender's front door until this past exhilarating hour spent stroking the strings of this beautiful instrument, her life seemed like a lovely dream, full of new and exciting things. American things. And such wonderful things: her small private bedroom at the end of the upstairs hall, a whole library full of books, the baby.

And now the harp, and the exquisite sounds she could make on it. She resisted an impulse to pinch herself. Surely she would wake up suddenly to find herself back in the dark, oppressive streets of her village in Schleswig. Nothing this wonderful could really be true. Nothing like this could last.

The door closed quietly behind the professor, and Erika leaned her forehead against the wood and closed her eyes. Oh, so much to do! Learn the English. Save her money to buy more books. Study hard, and...and one day soon she would be a real citizen of America! If she worked hard, God would surely make it possible.

She darted into the parlor, carefully stacked the cups and saucers on the tea tray and headed for the kitchen.

Jonathan lifted the rotting underbrush away from the creek bank with his walking stick and inspected the spongy ground underneath. He sank one end of the sturdy oak cane into the mud, withdrew it and watched the hole fill with slimy green ooze.

He knew what it would look like under the microscope—*Vibrio cholerae*. Cholera bacillus. He'd already taken samples from a dozen similar Plum Creek sites that lay downstream from the privies and livestock pens on farms outside town. Today he'd spent all afternoon talking to the property owners, trying to get them to understand. If only he could convince them to move their animals away from the creek drainage basin. The waste matter was contaminating the drinking water.

He'd talked himself into a lather at each farmstead and run into a brick wall of ignorance every time. "If you don't want your children to sicken, keep your outhouses and your goats—or cows or sheep or horses—at least one hundred yards from the creek."

"Bull chips, Doc," Cyrus Peck had countered. "Doc Chilcoate says there ain't no such thing as back-teer-uh. 'Sides, he can cure most anything with that Health Elixir of his."

Jonathan ground his teeth. It did no good to point out that "Doc" Chilcoate was the furthest thing imaginable from a trained physician. The man was a slick charlatan with a gift for gab and a medicine factory in his cellar. He'd purchased two buildings on Main Street with the profits from his tincture of ground chili peppers, molasses and watered applejack.

Jonathan's temples pounded with the familiar late-afternoon headache. Just one more mile and he'd go home and drink some strong coffee.

How many miles had he walked this summer? Fifty? A hundred? And for what? He'd started in midspring, after he read the journal article about cholera epidemics in the East. After Tess's death, he'd increased his woods rambling just to keep himself from going to pieces. He tried to put his anguish, his restlessness, to good purpose—preventing disease from decimating Plum Creek.

But he was failing. At least the antagonists in this battle were himself and Rutherford Chilcoate, not himself and God, as he had felt when he fought to save Tess's life.

Pain zigzagged across his forehead. He had lost the battle for Tess, and he was losing this one, too.

He pivoted and reversed direction. By the time he tramped back into town it would be dusk. In the cloying heat, sounds were magnified, his nerves stretched taut. His body pulsed with pain. With fear.

And with need.

He halted. *That was it,* he realized. That was the real reason he was reluctant to return home. He was afraid to see the light, quick movements of the young woman who inhabited his house and, lately, his unwilling thoughts. Afraid to watch her hands smoothing her apron or fluttering against the baby's soft, rumpled blanket. Afraid to hear her voice humming a low, breathy melody as she dusted the library books and shook out the nursery bedding in the morning sunshine.

Afraid to want her.

It will pass, he said to himself. *It is but the body's hunger, and it will pass.*

He set off again, retracing his path back to town. His head pounded at every step. *Soon,* he promised himself. Like the headaches that afflicted him with such regularity, his longing for Erika would ease, one way or the other. If all else failed, he would send her away and put the baby on a ship bound for Scotland, as he'd originally planned.

And likely sooner than later. He hadn't been sleeping, couldn't seem to keep the slim girl with the crown of honey-colored braids out of his mind.

Clenching his jaw against the relentless, racking ache in his skull, Jonathan quickened his pace. It was only a matter of time before he would reach the breaking point.

By the time he returned to town, the sun had drooped behind the purple hills, leaving the hazy, suffocating, still air of summer twilight. The streets of Plum Creek, even the shadowed lanes between buildings, shimmered with heat waves. He loosened another button of his linen shirt and rolled up the sleeves.

A low, droning sound, like the buzzing of bees, reached his ears as he stepped onto Chestnut Street. A block ahead the roadway seethed with townspeople.

The crowd moved away from him, turning down

Maple, and Jonathan quickened his pace. They were following something.

The voices, as he drew closer, rose in angry, strident tones. "Don't let the bastard get away," someone yelled.

My God! It looked like a lynch mob!

Jonathan began to run.

Erika drew back the lace curtain to see what all the noise was about. Townspeople crowded through the gate and onto the lawn, pushing up the porch steps. She gasped and drew back.

An irregular pounding noise on the veranda made her peek out again. Silhouetted against the glow of the setting sun was a slim form, bent almost double over a sturdy oak stick he used to support his weight. He dragged up the last step and hobbled toward the door. Blood soaked his trouser leg.

Erika yanked the door open. The boy was about fourteen with straight, dark hair that hung to the shoulders of his ragged flannel shirt. A braided deerhide belt held up his pants—many sizes too large for his slight frame. An Indian boy, she thought. And he was hurt.

His wary black eyes met hers. "Need doctor," he said through clenched teeth.

"I am sorry. Doctor is not here."

"Need bad."

Erika could see that. His lips twisted in pain and his eyes glittered. It was plain he was in agony.

"Why are these people here?"

"They follow me," the boy said. Sweat stood out on the olive skin of his forehead.

"Why?" she pursued.

"Say I steal horse. Not true."

Erika looked past the boy to the crowd milling on the walkway, the men's boots trampling her irises. She stepped out the doorway.

A needle of fear pricked her belly. "Go in," she said to him. "Go! Quick!"

She moved past him to face the crowd. In the front rank she recognized the mayor's wife, Tithonia Brumbaugh, puffed up like an angry hen. At her side hovered Mary Zabersky from next door and some of the other ladies she'd seen leaving the Presbyterian Church after Sunday services.

The short, burly man next to Tithonia was the mayor, she guessed. Behind him, eight or ten men milled about talking loudly among themselves and leaving huge footprints in the garden bed.

"What you want?" Erika said as calmly as she could.

"We want that renegade Injun," someone yelled.

Erika squared her shoulders and stepped to the edge of the veranda. In the dusky half-light the upturned faces looked like pale round apples of giant proportions.

"The boy is hurt," she said.

"He's a damn horse thief! Send him out."

Erika searched the gathering for the man who had spoken. "Ah, Mr. Valey. How do you know this?"

The mercantile owner shuffled his feet. "I just know. Whole town seen him ride in right down Main Street, bold as you please. But that horse wasn't his. No Indian coulda owned an animal like that."

"That does not mean he stole it," Erika responded. She had to raise her voice over the angry grumbling.

"I say it does," a woman called out.

"Me, too," another voice chimed.

Erika fisted her hands and deliberately propped them on her hips. "Wait one minute. If you have proof, then get sheriff. Otherwise—"

"Don't need no proof with an Injun, little lady. Don't need the sheriff, neither." The man cleared his throat and spat into her flower bed. "Just give us that thievin' kid and we'll clear out."

Erika stared at the tall, lanky figure. "No. I will not give him."

The man, one of the clerks at Mr. Brumbaugh's bank, jammed his hands into his jacket pockets. It occurred to her he might be carrying a pistol, and her heart rocked into a crazy rhythm.

"Is wrong what you do. This is America. You accuse boy because he is different. Indian. But have no proof. In America, must have proof. Must have justice."

"The hell we must! The kid's seen ridin' a horse too big for his britches. That's enough for me, right, mayor?"

Plotinus Brumbaugh hesitated until his wife jabbed an elbow into his ribs. "Why, uh, yeah. I guess so."

Erika's stomach lurched. She had seen such things in the old country. Men chased, beaten for no reason other than that their heritage or their religion was different. It made her feel sick.

She steeled herself to speak. "You are little men," she said. Her voice rang out in the silence. "Bullies who chase an injured boy. Is wrong. *You* are wrong." She pressed her lips together to keep them from trembling.

"Who's gonna stop us?" a raucous voice shouted.

She gazed at the crowd, and her heart quailed. She waited a long minute until she could speak, and in that moment a commotion at the back of the crowd riveted her attention.

Jonathan reached the edge of the gathering and shouldered his way forward through the mass of sweaty humanity that spread over his front yard. Erika stood on the porch, her face tight, eyes snapping.

Behind her, the front door stood open. What the hell was going on?

She looked out over the crowd but did not see him. "I will stop you," she said.

"Sure ya will, honey," someone called.

"The boy came to doctor for help. If he has done wrong, sheriff will come to take him. Not you. I will not let you."

Jonathan groaned inwardly at the resolve in her voice, the stubborn set of her chin. Still, he had to admire her for standing up to them—a mere young woman facing a mob of angry townspeople. He moved forward.

"Now, we want that Injun boy, miss, so you just stand aside and let us—"

Jonathan grabbed the speaker by his shirtfront. "You set one foot on my porch, and I'll beat the living hell out of you."

"Now, wait a minute, Doc. All we want—"

"I don't care what you want. Get off my property." He flung the man toward the gate. "All of you," he said. "Go home."

Plotinus Brumbaugh laid a restraining hand on Jonathan's arm. "Hold on, there, Jon. I'm not at all sure you want to harbor a criminal in your—"

Jonathan shook free. "Don't think for me, Plotinus. Just take this rabble and leave."

"Well, sure, Doc, if you say so."

Jonathan caught and held the mayor's gaze until the older man dropped his eyes and stepped back.

"Okay, Jonathan. If that's the way you want it. Come on, folks, let's go."

Jonathan took the porch steps two at a time. "Where is he?" he said to Erika as he strode past her.

"Inside house."

"Bring a lamp." He disappeared into the darkened front hall.

Chapter Ten

Erika held the kerosene lamp above her head and watched the doctor run his hands along the Indian boy's leg. "How did this happen, Samuel?"

The boy stiffened on the examining table as the doctor reached his thigh. "I walk across bridge. Buggy wheel ran over my leg."

"Hmm. Broke the femur. Erika, get some soap and hot water."

Erika set the lamp down and started toward the door of the tiny room.

"And bring a flatiron," he called after her.

Her skirt swished against his calf as she spun away. The instant she was gone, he slit Samuel's trouser leg and pulled off the blood-soaked denim. The lower half of the boy's leg jutted at an odd angle. He'd have to use Buck's extension to set it.

"Your brother know where you are?"

"Yes," the boy answered. "He will come for his horse tomorrow."

"Where'd you hide it?"

"In your barn."

Jonathan nodded. "I need three days to fix your leg, Sam. You can stay in the barn."

"One day."

"Three. I've got to put it in traction using a heavy weight. You won't be able to ride."

"I will ride."

"No, you won't. When Micah comes for you, we'll rig up a travois. Should hold till you get to the reservation."

Erika returned with the water. The boy closed his eyes and Jonathan worked quickly, sponging off the blood and dirt, then running adhesive tape down both sides of the leg and under the foot. He attached the flatiron to a strip of clean linen fashioned into a bandage. "The weight will straighten out your leg muscles, Sam. Then I can plaster it so it'll heal evenly."

"I make trouble for you. For her."

Jonathan caught Erika's startled gaze. "I'm getting used to it." He looked steadily into Erika's eyes for a long moment, then pulled his gaze back to Samuel. "Seems to me I end up setting one of your bones about every two years."

He taped the bandage firmly in place. "And Miss

Scharf here seems to attract trouble like honey draws bees. We will both survive.''

He chuckled at the expression on Erika's face. Her eyes flashed fire, but her lips curved into an embarrassed half smile. She was proud and stubborn as well as courageous and dangerously outspoken. He'd heard enough of the shouted comments in his front yard to know that she wouldn't have backed down without a fight.

''Just what would you have done if one of them had tried to force his way into the house?'' he inquired.

Erika studied the tops of her shoes. ''First I kick hard in shins,'' she said in a low voice. ''Then I get broom and...'' She pantomimed whacking the weapon at an imaginary enemy.

Jonathan laughed out loud.

''Is not for laughing,'' she snapped. ''In old country, have much need for strong brooms!''

At the look in her eyes, he sobered. ''And, it would seem, here in Plum Creek, as well. I'd guess you made a few enemies today.''

The light in her eyes dimmed, but she raised her chin. ''Does not matter. They were wrong. Not American way.''

Jonathan nodded. ''You'll see a lot of things done in America that are not the 'American way,' Erika. One example of that is lying here with a broken leg.

I'm not sure how far you'll get trying to fight injustice with a broom.''

But he understood her dilemma. He fought exactly the same battle with farm owners in the county who pigheadedly refused to move their privies and stock pens away from the town water supply. He wished he could take a broom to that problem.

"Sam, we'll get you up on some crutches and I'll help you out to the barn. Erika, bring some blankets, would you? And some oats and an apple from the kitchen for the horse.''

He'd go out later and take the boy some supper and sit with him. Guard him, in case any of those ruffians returned.

But instead of a broom, he'd take his revolver.

Erika stared out her bedroom window at the round, gold moon hanging like a lantern in the inky sky. Unable to sleep, she mentally reviewed the day's list of new English words. Plaster of Paris. Arpeggio. Succotash. Bigotry. She spelled each one and tried to remember what it meant.

Succotash was easy. Mrs. Benbow had served it at supper, along with cornbread, which she called johnnycake, and lamb stew. But after helping the doctor set the Indian boy's leg, she'd been too exhausted to eat. The housekeeper had excused her from kitchen duty and sent her up to bed.

The baby had nodded her tiny head almost immediately after her evening feeding and now slumbered peacefully in the nursery next to Erika's room.

Marian Elizabeth was such an exquisite creature, with her feathery fringe of dark hair and deep blue-green eyes, like a fairy child left by the elves. Erika could not imagine life without her soft, contented cooing sounds, the clear, round eyes gazing up at her with such trust. Whenever she entered the room, the baby looked up and actually smiled at her! It was a miracle—this house and the sweet baby girl who smelled of laundry soap and milk and the lavender sprigs Erika used to scent her garments. She wanted never to leave.

But in protecting that injured boy today, she knew she had made an enemy, and a formidable one at that. Tithonia Brumbaugh was the mayor's wife. Erika hadn't wasted time thinking about the issues. She had acted automatically because she felt inside it was the right thing to do. She'd been shocked at the surprise and hostility in Tithonia's sharp black eyes.

And, as president of the Presbyterian Ladies Quilting Circle, Tithonia was sure to influence the others. Just this evening, Mr. Zabersky's young daughter, Mary, had hastened past Dr. Callender's gate with barely a nod.

Marian Elizabeth gave a tentative cry, and Erika came instantly alert. But in the next few moments, the baby settled and Erika closed her eyes. She tried to chase away the image of Mrs. Brumbaugh's flushed, set face, but her thoughts wheeled about her brain like chaff tossed in a wind. An inner instinct told her she should not have challenged Tithonia face-to-face, and in public.

Dr. Callender said it was a thing called bigotry that made the mayor's wife and her ladies act the way they did toward the Indians and the two Chinese families who lived in a crude shack behind the livery stable. It was like the prejudice she remembered from the old country. She was sickened to find it here in America as well. She would never accept it, would speak against it every chance she got—no matter if it did make enemies.

She wanted nothing more than to be part of this wonderful land, to be an American, to *belong*. But she would not trade acceptance for discrimination against others.

It would be harder the next time, Dr. Callender had said at supper. *"Each time your integrity will be put to the test. Each time your soul will be pulled in two directions—to fit in or stand outside. Alone."*

She wondered how he knew these things. He was a man of high standing in the community, a physician who was looked up to, respected. But there was no mistaking the authority with which he spoke.

And, she recalled with a queer flip of her heart,

she would never forget the flicker of admiration in the doctor's ordinarily expressionless gray eyes. With a start she realized she valued that look more than any word or gesture of welcome from Tithonia Brumbaugh, or even the mayor! She longed to see that warmth, that approval, in Dr. Callender's gaze. In fact, she thought as a guilty wave of heat washed over her, each time his eyes met hers, whether over a vegetable dish passed at dinner or a basin of plaster mix in the surgery, a voice seemed to speak to her from far off, and she stopped breathing to listen.

Perhaps Mrs. Brumbaugh was right—not about the Indian boy, but about being alone in a house with a man who had lost his wife, a man who made her heart jump whenever he looked at her.

Erika sat bolt upright in bed. She must not allow this! If she was…what was the word, compromised? If she was compromised, she would have to leave.

And if she left, it would mean she would no longer have Marian Elizabeth to love and care for, could not play beautiful music on the harp downstairs in the front parlor, would not sleep in privacy in her very own bedchamber.

"Well, so be it," she breathed into the hot, still night. *I will not let my heart spin this way and that when the doctor speaks or glances at me.* She would be—she searched her brain—impervious.

At the soft chiming of the clock at the foot of the

staircase, Erika settled back and purposefully closed her eyelids. *Just one thing, Lord,* she prayed. *Please, please do not let him send the baby away to Scotland. I will do anything to stay by her side. Anything.*

In the morning Jonathan returned to the barn and found it empty. The boy was gone, and the big roan as well. He swore out loud.

Damn fool kid. How far could he get with a fractured thigh? He'd half a mind to saddle Scout and go after him.

On the other hand, he reasoned, considering how town sentiment ran these days, an injured Indian boy was probably safer on his own ground. At least he'd be protected among his own people.

Jonathan wondered who had run him down. A buggy, Samuel had said. Ever since Tithonia Brumbaugh had badgered her husband into purchasing a runabout when he was elected mayor, every businessman in town drove some kind of buggy.

Anger boiled hot inside him. When he found who it had been, he'd give him a good thrashing.

He shut the barn door with a decisive thunk and stomped up the back stairs, through the already stifling screened laundry porch and into the kitchen. Erika looked up from the stove where she stood heating a nursery bottle of milk in a saucepan of water.

"He's gone," he announced.

"I know. I hear the horse before sun rises."

"You heard him?" Jonathan exploded. "Why the hell didn't you stop him? Great Scott, that boy can't ride with his leg in plaster!"

Erika slid the pan onto the warming shelf. "I call out from window upstairs, but another man, an Indian, is with him. He makes a sign like so—" she slashed her hand in the air "—and I am quiet."

Jonathan expelled a swift breath. "That's Micah, Sam's older brother. He hates the white man. He'll rip that cast off Sam's leg and cripple him for life." He paced around the kitchen table as Erika watched.

"I'll have to go after him," he muttered. "Talk to Micah."

Frustration twisted his stomach. "Nothing, nothing has gone right!" he burst out. "Not since—" His voice broke off.

"Is not true," Erika remarked, keeping her back to him. "You have health. Life. You have beautiful baby daughter. A home. Many people have not so much."

Jonathan stared at her slim, straight back, the floppy bow of the white apron tied about her waist. What an exasperating young woman! She was right, of course. But the knowledge only fueled his fury.

"I no longer care about my life." He barely restrained himself from shouting the words. "Or my health. Or even my daughter!"

Very slowly Erika turned to face him. "Then you are very foolish man. Selfish man."

"So I am," Jonathan acknowledged, his voice shaking. "A crazed idiot on one fool's errand after another—arguing about creek drainage so a bunch of hotheaded, ignorant bigots can avoid an epidemic, setting Samuel's leg so he can walk into town for another bushel of corn to feed his hungry family and get run over. Or maybe next time they'll lynch him! You are right, I am a fool."

"No," she countered in her quiet voice. "You are not. But stubborn, yes. And hurt."

Stung, Jonathan wanted to shake her until that maddeningly steady look in her blue eyes turned to terror. He clenched his fists. "And opinionated, I suppose," he growled.

"Yes," she echoed. "Opin-ion-ated." She pronounced the word with care.

That did it! "Miss Scharf, you are improving your vocabulary at my expense!"

Her eyes widened. "Oh, no, Dr. Callender. I look up all these words before."

And then, unbelievably, she laughed. The low, musical sound increased his anger. She was laughing at *him. By God, he wouldn't allow...*

But, he admitted deep down inside, she was right. Again. He *was* hurt. And stubborn and selfish and, well, even opinionated. His anger, his dissatisfaction with his life, his unease, were misplaced. The insidious feeling of having somehow lost his center was because of Tess. The seething fury was his reaction to loss.

A wave of desolation overwhelmed him. He'd struck out against fate the only way he knew how, but his efforts had accomplished nothing. A black pit yawned inside his soul. The anger merely kept him feeling alive, and he clung to it for that reason.

He had to give it up. It was destroying him.

She was destroying him. She forced him to look at himself, and he didn't like what he saw.

Erika spun toward the stove. Lifting the bottle of warm milk from the stove, she wiped it dry with a tea towel and moved past him.

"I am apologizing for my words," she said as she brushed through the hinged Dutch doors.

Jonathan opened his mouth, then snapped his jaws shut. He'd be damned if he'd forgive her. She had an uncanny ability to strike home with a remark and then drive the blade in deeper.

"But..." Her voice floated to him over the sound of her footsteps ascending the stairs. "You are most wrong not to care about daughter."

"And you, Miss Scharf," he called after her, "are wrong to speak out to your employer about such matters!"

She was out of hearing. He muttered the words

over again to himself and then slumped into a hard-backed wicker chair, propped both elbows on the kitchen table and bowed his head onto his folded hands. No, she wasn't wrong. Indiscreet, perhaps. Unwise. But not wrong.

He wasn't such a fool that he couldn't see her intent. She was trying to help, trying to get him to come to terms with the fact that he had responsibilities. To the townspeople. To his daughter. To himself. The audacity, the sheer courage it took for her, a penniless, uneducated immigrant woman, to speak out to him as one human being to another made him shake his head. He wondered about her—not as a female, though she was certainly attractive in that way, but as a person.

What kind of woman would risk speaking the truth to the man who held her purse strings?

Uneducated or not, Erika Scharf was a woman of spiritual depth and uncommon courage. And in a place such as Plum Creek, a town full of meanness and prejudice, in the wider world such as it was today, with its falsehood and opportunism and bitter rivalries, how would she survive?

Worse, living under the same roof with him, a man who ached with need for a woman... God help them both.

Erika opened the front door and stepped back quickly as Tithonia Brumbaugh propelled her husband through the door and into the main hall. "We want to see Jon—Dr. Callender. Right away," the buxom woman demanded. "Don't we, Plotinus?" She yanked on her husband's arm.

Erika blinked. "Good morning, Mister Mayor. And missus."

"Right away!" Tithonia repeated.

"Doctor is not yet in office," Erika explained. "Has not yet had his break—"

"Well, my dear, you'd better go fetch him. This has gone on long enough." The white lace fichu at her breast trembled in agitation. "Hasn't it, Plotinus?"

"What? Oh, yes, my dear. Quite long enough."

The mayor's wife made shooing motions with her gloved hands. "Hurry up, girl!"

Erika pivoted and flew upstairs, skimming down the upstairs hall until she came to the closed door of the doctor's bedchamber. She hesitated a moment, trying to collect her thoughts.

What had gone on long enough? Had Tithonia found out about her harp lessons with Mr. Zabersky? Or had she perhaps discovered Erika had begun attending the Methodist Church evening service on Sundays instead of the Presbyterian morning church gatherings, which the mayor and his wife attended?

Surely freedom in America included choice of one's religious preference?

She tapped on the door, and it swung open. Jonathan stood before her in a rumpled white shirt, open at the collar, the sleeves rolled up past his forearms. His dark hair looked as if he had combed his fingers through it. The sight of the bare skin at the base of his throat sent an odd pang to her midsection.

"Excuse, please, Doctor. You have patients downstairs."

His usually impassive eyes hardened into hard gray slate. "At this hour? Is it an emergency?" He reached behind him for his coat and started to draw it on.

"Is the mayor," she whispered. "And Missus Mayor."

"Ah. In that case…" He tossed the black serge garment onto a chair and started down the hall, unrolling his shirtsleeves as he descended the stairs. Erika stole quietly after him, one step at a time. At the first landing, she halted. If she peeked around the corner, she could just see the edge of Tithonia's voluminous green sateen skirt.

"Tithonia. Plotinus. To what do I owe the honor?"

"Now, Jon, you know why we're here."

"No, Tithonia, I don't. Are you ill? Plotinus?"

"Certainly not," Tithonia snapped. "Not since my Jenny was born have I needed a doctor."

"Well, then?"

Erika crept forward until she could see the trio.

Plotinus shifted uneasily on the balls of his feet. "Uh, could we talk in your office, Jon? It's a matter of some importance."

"If it's about that Indian boy, he is with his people, miles from the valley. I rode up there yesterday and found them at their summer camp."

The mayor coughed. "It's not about them Injuns, Jon, though God knows I wish they'd stay away from town. Makes the folks nervous when they're about. Why, just last week—"

"Plotinus," the mayor's wife interrupted, "don't wander. Jonathan, we wish to speak to you in private."

"Of course." Jonathan ushered the couple into his study. "Erika," he called over his shoulder, "ask Mrs. Benbow to bring some coffee, would you?"

The door shut with a click, and Erika headed for the kitchen.

The minute Erika entered the warm, pleasant-smelling room, Mrs. Benbow seized her arm. "What're those two wantin'?"

"Coffee," Erika answered.

"For starters, that is." The housekeeper sniffed.

"What's so hush-up they need to be private, I wonder?"

"You were listening!" Erika said, aghast.

"'Course I was. I've got an idea what this is all about, I have." The housekeeper gave Erika a speculative look. "Seems Mary Zabersky, Mr. Zabersky's daughter—the one that plays the piano—belongs to Tithonia's quilting circle."

Erika listened with half an ear while she piled cups and saucers and a plate of freshly baked raisin scones onto a silver tray.

"Up to meddling is what I think," the older woman added. "Just you wait and see."

Erika fidgeted while the housekeeper poured the coffee into a white china server. She couldn't wait to take it into the doctor's study and hear at least a snatch of what was being said.

"And another thing," Mrs. Benbow continued in her raspy voice. "I wouldn't blame you if you did!"

Erika came to full attention. "If I did? Did what?"

The housekeeper settled the coffee on the tray Erika held and pushed her gently through the Dutch doors. "Walk slowly, my girl. You'll be able to hear more."

Hear what? Curiosity and dread warred in Erika's brain. And all at once she was certain.

Whatever mission had brought Tithonia Brumbaugh and the mayor to the doctor's house this morning had something to do with her. She would lose her employment. She was to be turned out into the street to fend for herself.

No, he wouldn't do that.

Oh, yes he would, a voice countered. *After you told him he was stubborn and opinionated? What were you thinking of, you foolish girl?*

Her heart turning to ice, she inched toward the study door.

Chapter Eleven

Jonathan turned to the mayor and his wife. "Now, then, Tithonia, what is this all about?"

Tithonia's bosom swelled. "Come, now, Jonathan. You mean to say you don't know? Why, the whole town is talking. Aren't they, Plotinus?"

"Oh, indeed, my dear. Indeed they are." The mayor hovered at his wife's shoulder as Jonathan settled himself behind his desk.

"Talking about what?" he inquired. He hadn't slept last night, had paced for hours about his room like a caged animal. Toward morning he had tossed himself fully clothed on the damask-covered double bed and dozed.

His head ached. His mouth felt dry. His patience with Tithonia Brumbaugh's nattering was wearing dangerously thin.

"Jon," Plotinus began in a hesitant voice. He

tugged at the tie constricting his fleshy throat. "Well, you see, Jon, it's like this. It's, uh, come to our attention that—"

"Just exactly whose attention is 'our' attention, 'Tinus? Yours? The employees at Rogue Valley Bank? Tithonia's?"

Plotinus blinked. "Well, um, you see, we feel— that is, the townsfolk—"

Tithonia jabbed a stiffened forefinger into her husband's ribs. "Stop stammering and spit it out!"

Precisely, Jonathan thought. To bring the matter to a head, he decided to help Plotinus out of his verbal wanderings. "It's about the other night, is that it?" he prompted. "When that Indian boy was run over?"

"Well, kinda."

Another jab of Tithonia's forefinger caused the mayor to catch his breath. "Yes. I mean, that's part of it, Jon." Plotinus's face flushed crimson.

"And the rest of it? Come on, 'Tinus, out with it. I've a long day ahead of me with the Bateson twins down with scarlet fever and Miranda Virostko about to deliver."

Plotinus's mouth opened and shut, then opened once more. A hoarse, strangled sound emerged. Tithonia waved her handerchief at him and took over.

"Jonathan, we know you're an honorable man."

Jonathan stared at the mayor's bulky wife. Honorable? Was he, indeed? He didn't feel so honorable after his troubling dreams about Erika these past few nights. Dreams in which she lay naked under him, soft and clinging. He felt he was being untrue to his wife's memory.

"And," Tithonia continued, "we all know the, er, situation you have here."

Jonathan sighed. Who in the hell was "we"? "Situation?"

"Come, now, Jon, you're a man, after all."

A bitter observation rose to his lips, but he bit back the words. Was a man who failed still a man? He kept his face expressionless. "And that means?"

"Oh, don't you see? Living here in this house together, she's sure to be compromised!"

"Don't be ridiculous, Tithonia. Adeline Benbow has kept house for me since she was widowed seventeen years ago. There's nothing com—"

"Adeline!" Tithonia's fichu twitched. "Who said anything about Adeline?"

Plotinus laid a pudgy, manicured hand on Jonathan's arm. "It's not, uh, Adeline we're concerned about. It's Miss Scharf."

"Erika? What about her? She's a bit of a trial at times, but she works hard and cares quite capably for the baby."

"But you're a bachelor!" Tithonia cried.

Jonathan shook off the mayor's restraining hand.

"I am no such thing." He struggled to keep the bitterness from his voice. "I am a widower, Tithonia. Not a bachelor. There is an infinite difference."

"But Miss Scharf is unmarried!" the mayor's wife blurted. "She is young. Unprotected!"

Jonathan's temples pounded. "From what, exactly, does she need protection?"

"From…from… Her reputation is at stake! Do you understand my meaning?"

"No, quite frankly, I don't. Miss Scharf is a perfectly respectable young woman, living in a respectable manner in a respectable household."

"With you!" Tithonia seemed to expand a size larger as Jonathan stared at her.

"Of course with me, as does Mrs. Benbow. This is, after all, my house." He took a long moment to draw in a long breath and expel it. "What is it you want, Tithonia?"

Plotinus cleared his throat. Tithonia resettled her voluminous sateen skirt and fidgeted with the knotted lace handerchief. "We want you to marry Erika Scharf."

Jonathan leapt to his feet. "*What?* Are you mad? Marry her! What on earth for?"

The mayor flinched as Jonathan loomed across the desk.

Tithonia held her ground. But, Jonathan noted, she

would not meet his eyes. She spoke into her lap, but the words were distinct.

"To salvage her social acceptability in Plum Creek, that's why. You must either send Miss Scharf away or marry her."

"Tithonia, I've known you a good number of years, and in all that time you haven't changed a bit. You are a meddling, hypocritical busy—" He broke off.

"Jonathan." Plotinus drew himself up to his full height. Even at that, he was still half a head shorter than his wife. "Jonathan, please."

"I'm sorry, 'Tinus. It's just that... Marry her? Good God, man, you can't be serious!"

"I, er, that is, we... Well, my dear, perhaps you should explain?"

"No." Jonathan cut Tithonia off before she could open her lips. "No need to explain. I suppose the Presbyterian Ladies Quilting Circle came up with this preposterous idea?"

"Most of the ladies agree. As Miss Scharf is alone, without friends or family to look after her, um, welfare, we feel it to be in her best interest to speak out on her behalf."

"Does Adeline Benbow know of this plot to save Erika from a bleak social standing in Plum Creek society?"

"Well, no. Adeline wasn't present."

"I see." Jonathan stepped from behind his desk. "Plotinus, take your wife home. Erika Scharf is quite capable of taking care of herself, alone or not. But, as it happens, she is under my roof, and therefore under *my* care."

"Exactly," Tithonia snapped. "Such an arrangement is quite improper."

"Plotinus, so help me—"

"Come, my dear," the mayor said quickly. "You've made your—our—point. The rest is up to Jonathan."

"You men!" Tithonia burst out. "You can be so pigheaded!"

Jonathan gazed at the mayor's wife, resisting the urge to throttle her. "I don't doubt that for a moment, Tithonia." He understood all too well the nefarious workings of a society-mindful female such as Tithonia Brumbaugh. He supposed Tess would have become the same over the years, given her family background, her privileged upbringing. It pained him to admit it, but Tess had the same tendency toward shallow mindedness he now observed in the mayor's wife.

Good God, what irony! Tess herself would have taken up Tithonia's cause! It didn't bear thinking about.

His hand on Tithonia's elbow, he urged the

mayor's wife to her feet. "Tithonia, Plotinus. I bid you good morning."

"But Jon—"

"Come back when you have the kind of complaint a physician can pay serious attention to." He reached for the brass doorknob and felt it turn in his hand.

The door swung open and Erika stood facing him, a loaded tray in her hands. "I bring coffee from Mrs. Benbow. Also some scones. You would like me to pour out cups now?"

Her gaze moved from him to Tithonia and Plotinus, and her face changed. "Something is wrong?"

Tithonia bustled forward. "Oh, no, my dear. Not for long, at any rate. Dr. Callender will put it to rights. Won't you, Jonathan?"

Erika's heart contracted. "Ah, I know already. He will send me away."

"Oh, no, Miss Scharf." Plotinus nervously patted his wife's sleeve. "Not send you away. Dr. Callender is going to—"

"Shut up, 'Tinus." Jonathan's voice rang in the quiet room.

Unable to breathe, Erika looked from the mayor and his wife to Jonathan. "Going to…what?" she asked in a quiet voice.

"We will discuss it later," Jonathan announced. "Leave the coffee, please, and show Mr. and Mrs. Brumbaugh out. They are just leaving." He lifted the tray from her trembling hands and set it on top of the medical journals spread haphazardly on his desk.

As she led the couple to the door, Erika caught the quick look of triumph that passed between the mayor and his wife. The expression on Tithonia's face reminded her of the way Papa's overfed tabby cat would look at her after it had slurped the thick foam from the milk bucket.

A bubble of unease expanded inside her chest. She longed to be a part of the town doings, make friends with Mary Zabersky and the other ladies, be included in their conversations. Maybe even join the quilting circle. But now she sensed an obstruction of some kind in her path. She didn't know why she was so certain, but the feeling was undeniable.

She knew it had something to do with her. She just didn't know exactly what it was.

But at the moment, none of Tithonia Brumbaugh's busymaking mattered. Doctor had not yet eaten, and the scones were growing cold. Erika jerked her chin up and returned to the study to serve the coffee.

Erika had three more harp lessons with Mr. Zabersky before she began to believe she wasn't dreaming. At the start of each session, her hands shook so violently she could barely keep them on the strings, but she ended the hour filled with a heady joy, anxious to start another series of practice exercises.

Keeping out of Dr. Callender's hearing grew easier as the Webbs and then the four Dettwiler children came down with scarlet fever. Then last night, after the grandfather clock on the stair landing had struck midnight, the doctor had been summoned to the Virostko farm. Mrs. Virostko's baby was coming.

Erika spent the morning washing diapers and hanging them out to dry in the hot sunlight, then scrubbed the kitchen floor, since Mrs. Benbow could no longer get down on her hands and knees. She raced through the chore, fed and changed the baby and laid her in the wicker cradle in the front parlor, where she gurgled contentedly. The infant drifted off to sleep when Erika began her practice on the harp.

An hour passed, then two. Erika kept an ear cocked for the sound of the doctor's horse, but morning stretched into afternoon and there was no sign of his return. She joined Mrs. Benbow for a late lunch at the kitchen table, folded the dry, sunshine-scented diapers and put them away in the chest upstairs. Then, with a final check out the front window for a horse and rider, she returned to the harp.

Such a glorious instrument! She could play for days without growing tired.

Jonathan turned away from the brawny, outstretched hand of Eben Virostko. "'Tweren't your fault, Doc,'' the heavyset man said in a low voice. ''Take the money.''

Jonathan pushed the man's hand aside. ''Hush now, Eben.''

''You saved my wife, Doc. I'm thankful for that. Guess the good Lord reckoned we had enough sons.'' He laid his palm on Jonathan's stiff shoulders.

The child had never drawn breath. Jonathan had tried everything he could think of. He'd dipped the tiny form into warm and then cold water, slapped its buttocks, massaged the chest with his forefinger, had even blown his own breath into the tiny, lifeless mouth. He'd worked an hour or more, lost track of time while Miranda lay on the cot, watching him. Finally she'd spoken to her husband.

''Stop him, Eben. Our baby's dead.''

A band of steel tightened around Jonathan's chest. The need to shout, even to weep, was so strong he swallowed convulsively, felt his aching throat constrict. A wave of weariness and despair closed over him.

''I'm sorry, Miranda. I'm so terribly sorry.'' It was all he could do to get the words out. And now Eben Virostko, a wall of solid flesh bursting the seams of his frayed work trousers and blue ticking shirt, again pressed the worn currency into his fingers.

''I can't take this, Eben. You know I can't.'' He stuffed the money into the pocket of the farmer's overalls, checked Miranda once again for any sign of fever and folded his medical bag with a snap. "I'll be out again in the morning to check on you."

He mounted Scout and set off for town, so bone tired he didn't care whether he got there or not. Death was always hard. But to lose a child... He could not comprehend the stoic acceptance of these sturdy farm people. Or perhaps they grieved, as he did, in private.

He kicked the gelding into a trot. The thought of his quiet study drew him forward, a sanctuary of peace and sanity in a world of inexplicable pain and loss. He needed soul-restoring silence and some brandy. A lot of brandy.

He needed to hear the soft, sensible voice of someone who was alive and well and whole.

Jonathan groaned out loud. He needed Erika. God in heaven help him, he needed to lay his head on her breast and release the anguish he held inside, let her soothe away the agony that gnawed his insides.

He heard the music when he came out of the barn. Harp music.

He was hallucinating, of course, but for just a moment...

The note pattern changed, then changed again. No, not his imagination. Someone was playing, practicing arpeggiated chords on the harp. Tess's harp!

Jonathan bolted up the back steps, tore through the

screened laundry porch and into the kitchen. The housekeeper jerked her attention away from the stove, and he saw her thin mouth open into a surprised O.

"Jonathan," she called after him. But he banged through the Dutch doors and into the front hall before she could finish.

What the devil was going on in his house?

Erika looked up as Jonathan strode into the front parlor. The harp rested against her right shoulder, and she held her breath, knowing it was obvious that she had been playing the forbidden instrument.

"Just what the hell do you think you're doing?" Jonathan shouted.

Out of the corner of her eye Erika caught a glimpse of a black bombazine skirt. Mrs. Benbow hovered just outside the doorway.

Erika swallowed hard. "I p-practice on harp."

"That, my dear Miss Scharf, is quite apparent."

The housekeeper poked her head around the corner. "That nice Professor Zabersky offered to give her lessons," she volunteered. "I advised Erika to accept."

"Lessons? On an instrument I specifically instructed you never to touch?" Jonathan addressed his remarks to Erika, not Mrs. Benbow.

Very slowly Erika returned the harp to its upright

position. After a moment's hesitation, she looked up at him. "Yes."

"Why? In God's name, why?"

"Because," she said, her voice almost a whisper, "is something beautiful, so beautiful that I must."

"Even when I forbid it?" Jonathan tried not to raise his voice. With his temples pounding as they were, he couldn't tell how loudly he was speaking.

"Yes, even then."

The rustle of Mrs. Benbow's skirt faded as she withdrew toward the kitchen, and in the next moment Erika heard the *whip-whap* of the Dutch doors.

Oh, God, what could she say to him?

The doctor's gray eyes hardened into granite. Hands clenched at his sides, he waited for her to explain. Twice she prodded her paralyzed tongue, but nothing came out. There was nothing she could say to him except the truth, but she didn't think she had the courage to utter it.

"I—I do not play harp to disobey," she began. Her voice shook, and her hand went to her throat. "Music helps the baby sleep when she is hot and fussy, but…"

She felt his eyes bore into hers, but she stiffened her resolve and went on. "But I do not do it for that, either. Or because Mrs. Benbow said music playing would help me to become lady. I do it…"

Erika brought her chin up and straightened her

backbone. "I do it because it is a lovely, fine thing, a thing that I want. For *me*."

Jonathan stared at the German woman who sat before him, her face upturned, her slim, capable-looking hands resting on the curved walnut harp frame. A light shone in the depths of her eyes, as if a candle glowed within. The color, he noted for the first time, was not just an intense blue; a band of deep violet ringed the iris, making her eyes startlingly beautiful. Arresting.

He knew he was staring. He tried to pull his gaze away and found he could not. He had never really seen her before this moment.

Under his scrutiny, her cheeks flamed to a deep rose, and she caught her trembling lower lip in straight white teeth. But her eyes, purple-blue in the waning light, looked straight into his with a kind of desperate courage. Jonathan's heart squeezed until he forgot to draw breath.

Without a word, he spun on his heel and walked out.

Across the veranda and down the front steps he strode, his head on fire, his body shaking. His entire life was turning upside down, somersaulting toward an unknown physical and spiritual place. He could feel it in the pit of his belly, in his bones.

A flicker of joy nudged his heart, kindling a wild,

irrational hope for something he could not even name. It scared the living hell out of him.

It had nothing to do with Tess's harp, or even with Tess herself. For the first time since her death he did not seek out the narrow, woodsy path to the fenced cemetery plot where she lay. He avoided it, walking until exhaustion threatened to cripple his breathing, and then he turned toward home.

She was still sitting in the front parlor, rocking the baby in her arms. No lamps had been lit. Soft, deep shadows enveloped her slim figure.

Jonathan moved forward. She did not move, but watched him with widening eyes.

Lifting her hand, he stared down at the small, clean fingers and then gently laid her palm against the strings of the harp.

Chapter Twelve

"Cures everything, folks! Rheumatica, worms, even female troubles."

Erika craned her neck to see the owner of the melodic tenor voice, but the jostling crowd around her hid the raised speaker's platform from view.

"Genuine Peruvian oil of coca," the voice sang. "Eases pain, builds strong bones. No mother's medicine cabinet should be without—"

A guttural voice broke in. "Will it help crippled leg?"

"Why, shore it will, mister! Just rub it in twice a day! Step right up now and purchase your bottle."

She saw the hawker now, an animated, pudgy figure in a rumpled seersucker suit. A jaunty straw hat rode high on a thatch of red hair. He doffed it as he waited for his customer to make his way forward.

"Come on, son. Come on. Time's a-wastin'."

An Indian man pushed his way out of the crowd. Erika gasped as she recognized the face under the threadbare felt hat. It was the same man who had come for Samuel that night—the Indian boy's older brother. What was his name? Micah, that was it. Micah Tallhorse.

"How much?" he grunted.

"That'll be tw—three dollars, boy."

Micah dug in his shirt pocket and came up with three silver dollars.

The crowd murmured. "Hey," someone called out. "Where'd an Injun get that kinda money?"

"Stole it, most likely," a man's voice said.

"Stole it most certainly!" That from a woman Erika vaguely recognized. One of Tithonia Brumbaugh's quilting circle ladies.

Micah turned to face the crowd. "Not steal. Sell horse."

"Where'd ya get the horse in the first place?" This time the speaker was Nate Ellis. Erika knew he worked at the bank. What was he doing in the town park at ten in the morning?

She gazed about her. In fact, half the town had gathered around the public square. Rutherford Chilcoate's speech and his elixir certainly drew a crowd! At the moment, however, she wished the people would thin out so Micah could purchase his medicine in peace.

It was for Micah's younger brother, Samuel, she reasoned. She longed to ask about the boy's broken leg.

Micah turned back to the medicine vendor, his face closed. "Money good," he said.

Doc Chilcoate reached out his short arm to take the money when a woman's shrill cry stopped him.

"Rutherford Chilcoate, don't you dare accept that silver!" Tithonia Brumbaugh bustled to the front of the swelling knot of townspeople.

"The mayor's wife is right, Doc!" Nate Ellis yelled.

Three coins clanked into Chilcoate's palm, but before he could pocket the money, two men stepped up and pinned Micah's arms behind him.

"Wait just a darn minute," one of them growled. Erika recognized burly, red-faced Madison Lander, Mr. Valey's part-time grocery helper. He tossed a coil of rope onto the ground. Erika noted it was tied with twine in two places and still bore a price tag.

"Grab it, boys!" Madison yelled. "Let's get rid of that thievin' Indian once and for all!"

Doc Chilcoate blanched. "Now, wait a minute, gentlemen."

"Can't see the need, Doc," Madison retorted. Micah began to struggle, and Madison kicked the Indian's legs out from under him. "Damned Indian stole my horse last year. That's a hangin' offense in any book!''

Another man stepped forward and twisted Micah's arm behind his back. Together they forced the Indian to kneel.

Erika dropped her market basket and fought her way through the seething mass of bodies to the raised square. Without thinking, she stepped up beside Doc Chilcoate, grabbed the brown glass bottle of Health Elixir out of his hand and smashed it onto the cement.

The sound of shattering glass brought the crowd to attention. Talk died away, and suddenly she found herself confronting the angry faces of half the town. The worst was Tithonia Brumbaugh.

Surrounded by her quilting ladies, the mayor's wife thinned her lips into a grim line. Her eyes snapped sparks at Erika.

Erika took a deep breath. "You must stop!" she cried. "Is not right."

"Neither is horse thievin', little lady," a voice called from the thick press of bodies. Erika riveted her gaze on the crowd, hoping to locate the speaker.

"You must prove that man is thief before give punishment!" Her voice wavered.

Micah's desperate black eyes met hers and it gave her courage. "In America..." Her voice cracked. "In America," she repeated, willing her voice to

reach to the edge of the crowd, "rule is by law.
This—" she pointed to the rope coiled at Madison's
feet "—this is not law, just men who are angry."

Tithonia elbowed her way forward. "Erika Scharf,
come down from there! You're making a spectacle
of yourself."

Erika gritted her teeth. She didn't want to offend
the mayor's wife, or any of the other ladies. She
wanted to be accepted by them, longed to be part of
Plum Creek society. If she spoke out, opposed Tithonia and the others, she knew she would set herself
apart. She would always be on the outside.

Erika swallowed, and she made her decision. "I
cannot help spectacle. Must not hang a man, any
man, Swede or Indian or Jew, just because he is different."

"What are you, sis?" a man shouted. "Some
kinda lady lawyer?"

"Hell, no she ain't," Madison Lander yelled back.
"She's a German. She's not even a citizen!"

"Erika!" Tithonia hissed at her. "Stop this at
once!"

Erika ignored her. She seized on Madison's remark to draw attention away from Micah and the
rope.

"I will be citizen soon. I come from German village, yes. Where they beat men who go to other
church and leave them to die. This I have seen."

She paused to straighten her spine and draw a fortifying breath into her lungs. "All men free in America. Equal."

Out of the corner of her eye she saw Madison's gaze fall to the coiled rope at his feet. Erika raised her voice to keep the crowd's attention on her. "German. Norski. Indian. All equal!"

Madison leaned over to grab up the rope, and in that instant Micah broke free. He tore across the square, heading for the alley between Valey's Mercantile and the bank.

The crowd surged after him, but Micah had vanished. A puff of dust behind the bank told her he had already mounted and ridden off toward the hills. He was safe.

She turned to Rutherford Chilcoate, who stood speechless at her side. "Please forgive," she stammered. "I spoil your selling."

The vendor closed his gaping jaw. "You're right about that, Miss Scharf. But you're right about that other thing, too. Here, have a bottle of my elixir. It's on me."

"Erika, really!" The mayor's wife propelled herself onto the platform and grasped Erika's arm. "You simply must learn how to conduct yourself in public! If you do not heed my advice, you will be ostracized!"

Erika pulled her arm out of Tithonia's grip. "Os-tra-cized? What is that, please?"

"Shunned," the mayor's wife said. "Left out of proper society," she added, lowering her voice.

Erika's spirits sank. It was too late. She had already spoken out and "made a spectacle," as Tithonia put it.

But such a price to pay for acceptance, an inner voice cried. *Compromising my deepest beliefs. To belong, must I step aside and be silent while a wrong thing is done?*

Heartsick, she moved away from Tithonia, gathered up her wicker market basket and made her way toward Valey's Mercantile. The mayor's wife and the other ladies pointedly turned away as she passed.

The only person who spoke to her was Madison Lander, and what he said made her feel sick to her stomach.

"You ain't never gonna be a lady," he whispered as she passed. And then he added something else in his low, mocking voice.

"Indian lover."

Jonathan shut the sound of the harp out of his consciousness and tried to concentrate on Rutherford Chilcoate's words. The medicine vendor had sought him out at his office, an unprecedented event in the long, prickly relationship between the two men. Chilcoate enjoyed mocking the "newfangled" ideas Jonathan had introduced from his rigorous medical training in Edinburgh, and Jonathan openly disdained the medicine vendor's self-appointed role as a "doctor."

The two hadn't spoken a civil word in recent memory. So what, Jonathan wondered, was the man doing here in his office?

"Point is, Dr. Callender, it don't matter what you think of me, or my Health Elixir. We both know it's mostly spirits 'n molasses, but it don't do no harm that I can see."

Jonathan marveled at the innocence in the man's expression. Was he dissembling or merely unaware of the effect his concoction had on people? Old Mrs. Madsen, who lived alone at the edge of town, for instance. After three or four generous doses of Chilcoate's brew, the widow imagined her dead husband had returned for supper. While chasing a stewing hen in her chicken yard, the poor woman had fallen and fractured her elbow.

"Allow me to reserve judgment on that issue for the moment," Jonathan replied stiffly. *Good God, I sound pompous!* It was true Chilcoate nettled him with his fancy claims for his mixture and his spurious use of "doctor" in front of his name. But since the man had come to his office for a consultation of some sort, the least he could do was to be civil.

"What seems to be the problem, Chilcoate?" Jonathan tapped his fingers and tried to keep his mind on his visitor instead of Erika's harp exercises. Her playing, he noted, had progressed astonishingly considering how few lessons she'd had. Of course, every minute she wasn't tending the baby or helping Mrs. Benbow in the kitchen she filled with practicing. Where, he wondered, did she find time for her English studies? He knew she was up before dawn each morning; when did she sleep?

He rested his chin against his linked thumbs and focused on Rutherford Chilcoate's round, ruddy face.

"Oh, there's nuthin' wrong with me, Doc. Healthy as a horse." He tapped his chest with his meaty fist. "It's *your* problem I've come about."

"My problem?" Jonathan jerked his chin off his thumbs. "And what problem is that?" Surely Chilcoate wouldn't try to sell *him* a bottle of that mess he touted?

The older man tilted his head toward the sound of the harp. "*That* problem. Miss Erika."

Jonathan eyed him. Just what was he hinting at? Surely she wouldn't want any of Chilcoate's elixir! If she was ailing, she would come to him.

Or would she? He hadn't been exactly pleasant these past weeks, he acknowledged. Had he driven her into the clutches of this medical charlatan? By damn, if Chilcoate had laid a hand on her...

"What about Erika?" he snapped. "Out with it, Chilcoate!"

The portly man's eyebrows shot upward. "Hold on a minute, Doc. There ain't nuthin' wrong with the girl. Fact is, I quite admire her. Why, she stood her ground like a soldier, talked that snake Madison Lander down to a nub."

"She did, did she?" What the devil was the man talking about? Had Erika been involved in some sort of altercation in town?

Chilcoate cleared his throat. "But," he continued, "there's gonna be talk. A proper unmarried girl like her just can't go traipsin' around makin' speeches and steppin' on people's toes, even if—"

Jonathan half rose from his desk. "Making speeches? Just what the hell are you referring to?"

The older man goggled at him. "Why, I thought sure you knew about it, Doc. Everyone in town saw her."

"Saw her do what?" Jonathan almost shouted the words.

"Why, save that Indian fella's neck, of course. Whole town's buzzin' about it. Thing is, it looks kinda funny to some of them, the mayor's wife, in particular."

"Tithonia Brumbaugh? What does she have to do with this?" In the next instant he deduced the answer. Whatever gossip was being circulated about Erika, Tithonia was sure to have a hand in it.

Rutherford Chilcoate nervously recrossed his short, thick legs and tugged at his shirt collar. "Now, I don't hold much with women talk, but it's gone beyond that, Doc. I thought you oughta know. Some of the men—Mad Lander and the Ellis boy—well, they're callin' your baby's nurse a...a...Indian lover." He swallowed convulsively. "With emphasis on the 'lover.'"

Jonathan stared at him, clenching his fists so hard the knuckles ached.

"Now, I hate to see a young lady get ruin't by such talk, so I came to you private-like with a little suggestion."

"Just what is your interest here, Chilcoate?"

The older man raised his hands, palms up. "Only interest I got is seein' a fine young woman save her reputation. That's why I'm speaking to you, man to man. See, if somebody was to marry her, she'd be safe, so to speak."

Jonathan flinched. Tithonia Brumbaugh's exact words. He'd thought the mayor's wife was just over-wrought that morning she and Plotinus had come to see him. Tithonia had no problem imagining the worst in any situation. Now he began to see the sense behind her suggestion.

"Just who did you have in mind for this act of

chivalry, yourself?'' For some reason the thought of one of Rutherford Chilcoate's fat fingers touching Erika's skin made his blood boil.

''Oh, not me, Doc. I got a wife already, back in Missouri. I was thinkin' it'd have to be someone the town respects. In fact, I was thinkin' it'd have to be *you*.''

''Me!'' Jonathan sank into his chair and dropped his head into his hands. *Think,* he commanded himself.

''Rutherford,'' Jonathan said in a dull voice. He'd never before addressed the man by his given name, but the nature of the two men's conversation this afternoon seemed to warrant it. ''Rutherford, why did you come today? Why do you care what happens to Erika Scharf?''

''Because of what she said in the square this morning,'' the older man replied. ''About this bein' America, and men bein' equal. It kinda touched me right here.'' He laid his palm against his heart.

''You see, Doc,'' the sober-faced medicine vendor continued. ''My real name's not Chilcoate. It's Chilkowsky. Radzu Chilkowsky.''

Jonathan closed his eyelids. His senses reeled, and his temples pounded with the headache he'd felt building during Rutherford Chilcoate's visit. He needed some coffee. If Mrs. Benbow was busy, he'd grind the beans and boil the water himself—anything to help his mind clear.

Radzu Chilkowsky had come to offer advice: Give Erika the protection of his name. The damnable thing was the man was sincere in his concern for the young immigrant girl Jonathan employed in his household. Chilcoate's warning against the social consequences Erika was naively inviting must be heeded.

But marry again? He lurched to his feet, felt the blood pound savagely in his head.

Not until hell froze over. Every fiber of his being resisted the thought. He had failed before as a husband and would never, ever, risk it again. What's more, of late he had times when he was uneasy about his mental state. He was quick to anger, argumentative. Depressed.

Given his emotional turmoil, he wasn't a suitable husband for any woman, let alone one who deserved a chance at real happiness in her adopted country. Between his inadequacies as a man and the demands of his medical practice, he could never make a woman happy.

That left only two options: Send Erika away from Plum Creek or find someone willing to offer her his name. Neither prospect eased the ache in his chest.

He hadn't been surprised hearing Chilcoate describe how she had spoken out for Micah Tallhorse. Erika was fair-minded, conscientious and honest to a fault. Dangerously so, according to the medicine vendor's account.

Jonathan listened to the rippling notes of the harp exercise Erika was practicing in the front parlor. She went over and over the passage until she had it right. It was plain she was extraordinarily gifted in music.

He hated to admit it, but if she left, he would miss her, more than he would have thought possible in the short time she had been here. Even Mrs. Benbow, for all her crusty air of disapproval, had grown fond of the girl. Erika learned quickly and worked hard. The aging housekeeper even admitted Erika had "brought a beam of sunlight into her kitchen and had been God's true gift to that poor wee babe."

No matter, Jonathan resolved. He had to do something. He could not in good conscience simply toss someone as fine and spirited as Erika Scharf to the wolves. But keeping her on as his employee meant she would be shut out of respectable Plum Creek homes, or worse, forced to marry some ne'er-do-well who had the audacity to lay his hands on her.

His heart faltered. For her own sake, he acknowledged, the young German girl must leave his house. He dreaded confronting her with such a decision. All at once, his body felt heavy, his mind weighed down by misgivings and an odd sense of loss.

But for Erika's sake, he knew he had to act. What must be, must be. Before he could allow the thought to paralyze him, he wrenched open the door to his study.

A wave of sound met him—arpeggios cascading like a clear mountain waterfall. He shut his ears and forced his feet to move toward the parlor.

Chapter Thirteen

"Erika, come into my study, will you?"

Erika stood immediately and smoothed her slim hands over her dark blue skirt. "I check on baby first. Then bring tea?"

Jonathan sighed as she moved toward the parlor doorway. "No. No tea. Coffee, if it's not too much trouble."

She flashed him a pleased look, her wide mouth curving. "Is no trouble. Mrs. Benbow grind fresh this morning. I fix."

Jonathan barred her way. "On second thought, forget the coffee. I'll have a brandy. Come."

Her eyes widened into pools of violet. "But the baby…?"

"Now," he repeated. He'd lose his resolve if he waited. Better to get it over with. "I'll leave the door open. If the child cries, you will hear her."

One brandy would never be enough, he thought, watching the small, softly curving figure move ahead of him. Before the matter of what to do about Erika was settled, he'd no doubt drain the whole decanter. Maybe two decanters.

She perched on the edge of the brown damask consultation chair, her unease evident in the stiff set of her shoulders.

"Miss Scharf," he began. He cleared his throat and bent over the silver tray of spirits he kept on one corner of his desk. He splashed three fingers of Jarvis's into a tumbler, noting that his hand shook.

"Miss Scharf, is there anyone in Plum Creek, that is, have you met someone, a man, who..." He stopped as a wary look crept into her eyes.

"What I mean is...um...it's come to my attention that..." Lord help him, he couldn't curl his tongue around the words! He downed a double gulp of brandy. "Do you wish to stay in Plum Creek?" he blurted out.

The color drained from her face. Speechless, she stared up at him. Jonathan turned away and moved heavily to the window, clutching the tumbler of spirits. "The thing is, Erika, people are beginning to talk."

Behind him, her voice came low and clear. "I do not care about talk."

"I'm afraid it isn't that simple." He found himself

fervently wishing that it was, that Tithonia Brumbaugh and Rutherford Chilcoate would vanish in a puff of summertime smoke and leave Erika and himself alone. But in a town as close-knit and gossip prone as Plum Creek, he knew there were others who would take their place. Madison Lander, for one.

Jonathan swore under his breath and pivoted to face her, sloshing brandy over the rim of his glass. ''Whether you care about talk or not, you are vulnerable. You are young. Unmarried. Attractive.''

''I have done nothing wrong,'' Erika stated flatly. ''Nothing to make gossip. I think in America, prove first, then guilty? So, in my opinion, is not me but false-sayers who are wrong.'' She folded her hands in her lap and lifted her chin.

Jonathan groaned inside. He was beginning to recognize the gesture. When she stiffened her bearing that way, her heels were digging in. Attractive, yes. Vulnerable? Sometimes he wondered.

But she was intelligent and outspoken to a fault. God save him from women with opinions!

A faint tinge of rose touched her cheeks. She bent her head and Jonathan studied the curve of her neck, the crown of honey-colored braids that wound about her head. She was a beauty, he had to admit. He wouldn't blame any man for wanting her. He wanted her himself, he admitted. At night he lay awake, unable to get her out of his thoughts, aching with desire.

"You think I am attractive?" Erika said hesitantly.

"Well, um, that is..." He groped for words. "Yes," he said at last. "Most definitely."

She trailed the fingers of one hand over her forehead, down her cheek. "Truly?"

He nodded. Her color deepened. She smiled, frowned, then smiled again. The glow in her eyes made him forget what he had called her into his study to say.

Get hold of yourself, man! You're too old and too emotionally depleted to have a second thought about a woman, any woman. Even one as lovely and intriguing as Erika Scharf. Tipping the tumbler of brandy to his lips, he gulped twice and jerked his thoughts back to the issue at hand.

"Miss Scharf—Erika, would you want to stay here in Plum Creek? Permanently, I mean?"

"Oh, yes! More than anything. I want to take good care of baby and some day become citizen of America!"

He shook his head in disbelief at her innocence. No woman he had ever known had been so direct and so artless. But perhaps Erika harbored no social aspirations, as Tess had. An immigrant girl from Germany might not care whether she was the most fashionably dressed lady at a society event, might want nothing more than respectability and a roof over her head.

A flash of irritation nipped at him. He had spoken to Tess only once about her preoccupation with her appearance, her social status. Tess had merely shrugged her pretty shoulders and ignored him.

Jonathan kept his voice neutral. "Erika, what do you want for *yourself?*"

Her face came alive. "Ah, so much I want! To play music, but this you know already. I want also to make friends and speak good language. And—" She caught her lower lip in her teeth.

"And I like very much my bedroom upstairs. Is all my own and so quiet I hear birds at morning time. Very peaceful. Also, I like many books to read, and…and…"

"And?" Jonathan prompted. The girl wanted such simple things, so easily attained. Because of his privileged background, he had never considered how impossible such things as privacy and music lessons might seem to a penniless girl who was alone in the world.

But if that were the case, would she naively accept the attentions of the first man to offer her such things? How could he protect someone as vulnerable as Erika?

Find a husband for her, a voice within spoke. *A man who will take care of her.* Jonathan's breathing caught. He would have to arrange a suitable marriage and let her go.

He spoke over an unexpected tightness in his throat. "Would you want to marry?"

Her eyes widened. "You mean, leave baby? Leave this house?"

He nodded. Her face was so changeable, he marveled. She looked determined one moment, stricken the next.

"You could have your own house. Your own children."

"No," she said, quiet decision in her voice. "I would not marry."

A curious feeling of joy mingled with his frustration. He downed another mouthful of brandy. "There is no man you yet care for, is that it?"

As he said the words, he realized he hated the thought of her caring for someone. Until Rutherford Chilcoate's visit, he had been aware only of his own struggle to keep his mind off Erika. He'd never given a thought as to where Erika might put *her* affections. Now, as the silence hung in the warm summer dusk, he found himself giving it quite a bit of thought.

"No," she replied at last. "Is not the reason. I...I want to stay here, with baby and— With baby."

"But I'm afraid that solves nothing." God in heaven, would he have to dismiss her after all?

"You see, Erika, things cannot, um, must not continue as they are."

She looked at him with sudden, keen intelligence. "People think bad of me, like Missus Mayor says?"

He winced at the pain in her voice. "Some do, yes. But it will stop if you—"

"I must do what Missus Mayor asks? Then I am accepted? People will like me? Have friends?"

Jonathan's gut twisted. She certainly had a knack for boiling issues down to the bare bones. And ugly bones they were. Gossip. Social prejudice.

All at once he hated Tithonia Brumbaugh, the mayor, the townspeople of Plum Creek. Not only did they resist change, clinging to a dangerously outdated water system that threatened them all, but their small-mindedness excluded outsiders who did not conform to their narrow, entrenched ideas about right and wrong. Erika could not hope to win.

Erika raised her chin. "Do *you* ask this? Want me to leave, do what mayor's wife says I must?"

"Yes," he lied. "I ask it."

She was intelligent. She would see what she must do to survive. He waited for her acquiescence.

She met his eyes in an unflinching gaze. "Friends I will have, in time," she said in a quiet voice. "And people not say bad of me. But," she concluded with careful, clearly enunciated words, "I will do what best *I* think, not Missus Mayor."

Jonathan felt like cheering. The girl was silk on the outside, but inside—inside, where it counted—

her bones were made of steel! She was as stubborn, and as single-minded, as Tithonia Brumbaugh. A wave of admiration lifted his spirits. By God, Erika was a match for the mayor's hypocritical wife. He should send Erika to the next town council meeting!

"And," Erika added with a tremor in her voice, "I will marry what man I please or not at all. No man will know me without I want him to."

She rose without looking at him. "I hear baby cry."

"Erika, wait." He had heard nothing, not even Mrs. Benbow's usual pre-supper stirrings from the kitchen. He set the brandy glass down on his desk harder than he intended; the liquid slopped over onto the latest *Medical News*.

"I feed baby. Then I pack my clothes."

"No! Erika, listen to me. You mustn't leave. It isn't necessary—we'll find another way. I'll—I don't know. I'll talk to Tithonia."

"Will make no difference. Everything has already been said. Missus Mayor speak. You speak. Is not what I want, to leave house and baby, but you explain that I must do something, and so I do it. Please, may I have a little brandy?"

"Of course." He tipped the decanter and splashed a scant half inch into a small glass. Erika scrunched her eyes shut and downed it in one gulp.

Her eyelids flew open, and she sucked air into her

lungs. "So hot!" she rasped. Her forefinger traced a line from her throat to the center of her chest. "All the way going down, to here!"

Suddenly Jonathan knew what had to be done. He snatched the glass from her hand and poured another shot. "Here. Have another one."

This time she took a small sip, wrinkling her nose as she swallowed.

Jonathan addressed a short prayer to the God he'd thought had forgotten all about him, stiffened his resolve and drew in a deep breath.

"Erika, I am financially very well off," he said rapidly. "I own this house and the Cooper building, as well as estates in Scotland and a large farm in Pennsylvania. I want you to marry me."

She choked on the brandy. Tears swam in her eyes, and the ivory lace ruffle at her neck trembled. "What you say?"

"I want to marry you."

Erika struggled to slow her whirling thoughts. What was it doctor said? He wanted to... Had she misunderstood the English? Or dreamed it, perhaps?

Dazed, she aimed her glass of brandy toward the decanter set amidst the clutter on the doctor's desk, settling it with a click on the silver tray. No more spirits for her, she decided. They gave her such beautiful imaginings, too incredible to be real.

She noticed that he watched her every move, as if waiting for something, an answer to something.

I want you to marry me.

She jerked upright. Ah, no, it was no dream! He had said it twice. He wanted to marry her?

Oh, kind mother in heaven! He wanted *her*? Plain Erika Scharffenberger from Schleswig?

"Erika," he said gently. "May I have your answer?"

Answer? What could she answer? That she had loved him from that day in the front garden when he had clung to her, his body shaking with his grief? That there were chasms between them she feared would only widen with time?

"Erika…"

"Please," she said in a choked voice. "I am thinking."

"Thinking! What on earth is there to think about? This is the only solution that makes any sense. I can't auction you off like a side of beef! And I…well, I find I am not willing to send you away. You are…good with the baby, and Mrs. Benbow speaks highly of the help you provide. And," he added in a barely audible voice, "*I* need…that is, you are a fine young woman, Erika. I would be honored to give you my name, provide a home for you."

He ran his hand through his hair and frowned. "I

assure you, it would be a marriage in name only. I would not want to force..."

Erika forced her gaze upward to meet his. His eyes, like two gray stones, blazed with a hot light.

"Is not enough," she said.

"What do you mean, not enough? I'm offering you everything I own!"

"Some things you do not own. I want to love baby, like good mama does."

"You will be the child's legal mother from the moment you accept my offer to the day you die, Erika. No matter what happens, I promise never to separate you from the child."

Still she hesitated. If she was to enter into a covenant between the two of them, something deep inside her clamored to be spoken aloud.

"I want also some day to love man like...like a woman does."

She watched his pupils darken, felt her heartbeat quicken as he moved toward her and took hold of her arm.

"If you wish it." His voice shook. He was as frightened of such a momentous step as she was!

"Yes," she said with deliberation. "Some day. When time is right."

Erika's brain reeled. He was a good man, there was no question in her mind about that. She had watched him set that Indian boy's broken leg with steady, capable hands, saw him wince as his manipulation caused pain. She saw the respect he paid to the mayor and his meddling wife, even when his jaw muscle twitched in fury.

The townspeople sought Dr. Callender's opinion on matters that had nothing to do with medicine—schooling for their children, events abroad, which he kept up with through the foreign newspapers he read. And Erika recalled the offerings left at the back door by poor farmers, grateful for a prescription they could not afford, an extra visit, a birth. A bushel of new potatoes, an overflowing box of late Red June apples. One morning she had found three fresh trout wrapped in a blanket of damp moss. Micah Tallhorse had left them.

Yes, doctor was a good man. But there were other things. He did not attend church, preferring instead long solitary walks in the country with only his writing tablet and a hastily cobbled sandwich stuffed in his jacket pocket. He wore wool in the summertime—most odd—and preferred his linen shirts starched so stiff they crackled when she turned them on the ironing table.

He was separated from himself in some way, grieving for a wife not many months in her grave. More important, he seemed to care little for his own child, Marian Elizabeth. What kind of man was he on the *inside?*

She didn't know. But the truth was, she acknowledged, she would not in the least mind spending the next twenty years finding out.

"In the Methodist church!" the housekeeper spluttered. "Now, how are ye goin' to get that man to set one foot inside the place, even if it *is* for his own weddin'?"

Erika plopped her teacup onto the china saucer. She liked talking over her plans with Mrs. Benbow. The older woman shared her honest reactions, and Erika found invaluable the advice of someone who had managed the doctor's household in Plum Creek for twelve years.

"He will come, I think. Only way to sign records of marriage!"

Mrs. Benbow's lined face crumpled into a grin. "You're a canny lass, you are. Now, about your wardrobe."

"Wardrobe? What means wardrobe?"

"Why, your day dresses and gowns. Your trousseau, your night clothes and pretties."

"Trousseau," Erika breathed. "Such a fine-sounding word!"

The housekeeper sniffed. "Nothing fine-sounding or high quality to be found at Valey's Mercantile, I'm sure. That means a trip to the city or mail order from back East. 'Course, if you send away for your things, they won't arrive till after the weddin'. Which'll it be, my dear? Doctor's a generous man. He said to spare no expense."

"Oh, I could not leave baby for travel!"

"Mail order, then. Except for your weddin' dress. That's got to be special."

Erika rose to clear away the tea things. "I have only my black travel dress. Is silk, but so dark a color."

"'Twon't do at all," Mrs. Benbow snapped. "Mind you, I said special. And I happen to have just the thing in my trunk. Just you wait one minute."

She bustled past Erika and disappeared through the Dutch doors, her bombazine skirt swishing down the lower hall. In a few moments she returned, an ivory lace dress folded over her arm. The old woman's face beamed. "Just you look at this, lass!"

She spread the gown over the back of the tall kitchen chair she had vacated, and Erika gasped. The dress was a confection of ivory silk and lace, with wide flared sleeves, a simple square neckline and a voluminous gored and gathered skirt with a deep ruffle at the hem.

"Oh," she whispered. She brought her hand to her mouth. "Oh," she said again. "Is so beautiful!"

"'Course it is. I wore it at my own wedding twenty years ago."

"Oh, but I—I couldn't wear your dress!"

"And why not? I've saved it all these years, wishin' I had a daughter who'd wear it one day. Take it, lass. We can alter it here 'n there, narrow the sleeves, maybe add some lace here—" she moved her veined hand from the neckline to the hem "—and here. I saw one in Godey's almost identical except for the bustle. Didn't much wear 'em in those days, but we could add—"

"No!" Erika protested. "You are so kind to offer, but I could not change such a lovely dress."

"Well, suit yourself. You'll look a picture with your coloring. After your wedding you can put it away for *your* daughter."

Erika's mouth dropped open. "My daughter?"

"The baby, lass," Mrs. Benbow gently reminded her. "Marian Elizabeth. After next Sunday, you'll be her real and true mama."

Erika's heart took wings. *Marian Elizabeth Callender will be my daughter?* With reverence she caressed the soft ivory silk.

In three short days she would say some words, sign her name in the registry book and become the baby's mother!

She sat down suddenly. *And become Jonathan Callender's lawful wedded wife.*

"Why, what is it, lass?"

She couldn't speak, could only shake her head in joy and bewilderment. Tears stung her eyes. It was too much. Happiness such as she had never known coursed through her. She had wished for the moon, and it had been granted!

"Ah, wedding nerves, o'course." The housekeeper gave Erika's shoulders a squeeze. "Don't you worry, child. It'll all come right in the end. Just you put on this dress come Sunday, and let your heart take you the rest of the way."

Her heart. Her heart had already flown two or three times about the world since Dr. Callender—Jonathan—had proposed marriage. Shortly it would float earthward and settle forever in the large, gracious house on Maple Street in Plum Creek, America.

And there, God, if You are willing, it will stay forever.

Chapter Fourteen

By the following Sunday afternoon, Erika was so nervous she felt she would jump right out of her skin. The slightest sound sent her heart racing; even the soft *whip-whap* of the Dutch doors into the kitchen set her nerves on edge.

Her wedding dress, freshly aired, pressed and scented with rose petals, lay on the bed upstairs in her room while in the kitchen Mrs. Benbow fussed over Erika's hair with a heated curling iron.

"Such waves ye've got!" the older woman said. "And they've a mind of their own, for sure. It's like tryin' to curl crimped silk!"

Erika squirmed on the hard wooden chair. "I shouldn't have braided it this morning."

"More like you shouldn't have gotten up and milked that goat, my girl! The dry air's what's done it. Why, it must have been ninety degrees by breakfast time, and on this day of all days." The house-keeper continued to mutter as she fussed with the hot iron.

"The baby need milk," Erika replied matter-of-factly. *"Needed,"* she amended. And then she added, *"The* milk. Needed *the* milk." English, she reflected for the thousandth time that week, was full of pitfalls.

Like life, a voice added.

Erika felt the heat of the afternoon press in on her. Even at dawn, the air had hung heavy and still. The finches that usually twittered among the branches of the plum tree outside her window were silent, as if the first searing rays of the sun warned of the scorching day to come. The house, especially the kitchen, seemed to wilt into sleepy torpor as the day progressed.

She practiced out loud the various phrases Mrs. Benbow had suggested she might need today, especially at the reception that would follow the wedding ceremony. "Thank you very much...so happy to meet...to make your acquaintance..."

Tithonia Brumbaugh had insisted on the reception, had commandeered the Presbyterian church hall, across the street from the Methodist church where the ceremony would be held, and had volunteered the quilting circle ladies to serve refreshments. Erika could not envision a social gathering at which she and Jonathan were the guests of honor. The thought of being on display, watching her English pronunciation, her manners, the hem of the delicate lace dress, gave her stomach the flutters.

"Sit still, lass! You're a basket of twitches!"

Erika groaned. By five o'clock, when she would go to church with Dr. Callender—Jonathan, she reminded herself—it would be worse. Never in her entire life had she felt such fear, not even the day she boarded ship at Bremerhaven to sail to America.

Of what was she frightened? Surely not the great good fortune that had befallen her. She was blessed, truly blessed, to be marrying a man she cared for, a man honored in his community. A man who, she fervently prayed, could grow to care for her. At least up to a point. Erika recognized Jonathan's grief over his first wife; that would take time to ease.

"There, now," Mrs. Benbow pronounced with satisfaction. She laid the metal curling iron aside. "Let's have our tea, and then ye'd best don your petticoats, lass. 'Tis almost four."

But when the tea was brewed and poured out and a plate of the sticky buns Erika loved sat before her, she found she could not swallow a single bite. She took a few sips of her tea and watched Mrs. Benbow devour a bun.

The old woman gave her an appraising look. "More wedding jitters, have ye?"

Erika nodded, her throat suddenly tight.

"Well now, my girl. Since ye've no mother here, perhaps you'd like to talk a bit, about the wedding and all. And...afterward."

Erika's entire frame jerked to attention. Afterward! In her dazed state of mind, she hadn't gotten as far as *afterward*. Despite Jonathan's assurance of the continued privacy of her own small bedroom upstairs next to the baby's nursery, what would he expect on their wedding night? Even if it was to be a marriage in name only, would he want her in his bed?

She knew about coupling. But the questions she had were too complicated, too—what was the English word?—subtle to ask Mrs. Benbow. Besides, no one, not even the trusted housekeeper, would ever know the private agreement she and the doctor had made on the matter of intimacy.

"Thank you, no," she said, patting Mrs. Benbow's wrinkled hand where it rested on the tea cozy. "I am country girl—*a* country girl," she corrected. "I know all about such things as mating."

Such relief shone in Mrs. Benbow's face that Erika stifled a giggle.

"So be it, lass. Considering all those flowers you're always plantin', and milkin' that goat every morning, I should have guessed."

Ah, yes, Erika's inner voice spoke. *Plants I know about, and goats and making cheese and kneading*

*bread, and animals mating and bearing young. But
what do I know about men?*

And what, above all, did she know about this man
in particular?

The butterflies in her belly fluttered against her rib
cage, teased her spine. With shaking hands she gathered up the full skirt of her muslin chemise and
scooted off the chair. "I dress—*will* dress now." She
hugged the bosomy housekeeper until the stiff bon-
ing of the old lady's corset pressed hard against her
breast. "Thank you for everything," she whispered.

"I'll come help you with your corset, lass."

Puzzling over the choked huskiness in the housekeeper's voice, Erika headed for the stairs and the
second-floor room where her wedding dress—and the
start of her new adventure as Jonathan Callender's
wife—waited.

Jonathan pulled Daisy up before the large, graceful
house and stared at it as if he'd never seen it before.
It wasn't the same house he had brought Tess home
to after their hurried union and long train trip from
Savannah. It looked different. Brighter. As if someone had scrubbed the exterior with a stiff brush. The
colors looked sharper. Certainly the garden looked
different, but that, he knew, was because Erika spent
many afternoons on her hands and knees planting
things in the rich, black soil. Such an apparently art-

less blending of shades and shapes that it looked like one of those Impressionist paintings he'd seen once in Paris.

Daisy shook her head with impatience, and he released the reins. Descending from the buggy, he absently rubbed his shirtsleeve over the shiny black finish. He'd spent hours waxing and polishing it this morning, had skipped breakfast and noon dinner, in fact. Young Timmy Ellis had offered to do it for him, but Jonathan had refused. He'd flipped the boy a dime and said the task was a labor of love. Timmy had sent him a look of utter disbelief and skipped away, no doubt to spend his fortune at Valey's candy counter.

Ordinarily he would have hired the lad, but today he needed to keep his hands busy. Otherwise, he noted, they shook like the yellowing leaves of Ted Zabersky's quaking aspen tree. For some reason, smoothing the soft flannel rag over the buggy's paint calmed his nerves.

The last time he'd been so uneasy was before his first surgery at medical college in Edinburgh. "Here," the head surgeon had said. "You do it, Callender. Make a clean incision and remove this boy's appendix."

Odd that he hadn't felt this fear when he'd married Tess. But then, he'd scarcely had time to get his bag unpacked in Savannah before he was repacking it and heading west with a wife. Tess was always in a hurry.

Well, he wasn't hurried now. Far from it! He'd spent the long morning hours laboring over the buggy in which he would drive Erika to the church, and part of the afternoon tramping in the woods west of town. Whatever the outcome of this day, and the life that would follow, for better or worse, he would at least have the satisfaction of knowing he had provided a proper conveyance. In a way it was like sterilizing his instruments before beginning a surgery; proper preparation ensured at least a fighting chance for success.

By three o'clock he couldn't stand it any longer. He slipped in the front door and up the stairs to the master bedroom to dress for the wedding.

A single thought nagged at him. More than offering protection and a safe, comfortable home, he wanted to please Erika. He liked the woman. Wanted her, even. When she passed close enough that her scent reached his nostrils, he ached with desire. She smelled of lilacs and some subtle, musky spice. His head swam when she was near him.

The truth was, he wanted her to like him. Be content with him, with what he was and was not. Tess had been dissatisfied in some way he could never fathom. He did not want to disappoint Erika.

His terror at the prospect of another failure held in

rigid control, Jonathan entered his bedroom and began to unbutton his rumpled day shirt.

Dressed and ready at last, Erika sat by the open bedroom window, hoping a late-afternoon breeze would stir the hot, still air. The house was quiet. After lacing up Erika's corset, Mrs. Benbow had left for the church on the arm of Mr. Zabersky, who had extended the invitation after Erika's music lesson last week. In a single breath he had exclaimed over the housekeeper's sticky buns and offered his sevices as escort.

Erika smiled at the sight of the elderly couple, arm in arm on the street below, pushing the white wicker baby carriage ahead of them.

It seemed a miracle, all of it. She was to marry Dr. Jonathan Callender, and her baby daughter would be present at her new mama's wedding! Most miraculous was the way she felt deep down inside, beneath the folds of ivory silk and the stiff laced corset.

Dizzy with happiness, she rose to secure the diaphanous floor-length veil Mrs. Benbow had given her. It drifted to the toes of her simple buff-colored shoes, and the gentle tug of its weight tightened the combs securing the small circlet of Mr. Zabersky's white roses that crowned her head. She couldn't see her entire form in the small dresser mirror, but Mrs. Benbow had pronounced her "just perfect" before she left. Erika decided she would trust the older woman's judgment.

It was time to make her way down the staircase to the buggy waiting outside. She moved toward the hallway, but just as she reached the door, she turned back. For a long moment she surveyed the tiny room.

Then, lifting her chin, she stepped resolutely into the hall and moved forward to meet her new life.

Jonathan spoke in low tones to calm the restive mare. As always, Daisy was anxious to be off. "Just a few more minutes, girl, and then you can—" He broke off at the sight of a vision in ivory lace floating across his veranda and down the front steps. Unconsciously he straightened on the leather seat and swallowed hard.

Erika. My God, she was so beautiful it made his throat ache.

She moved toward him, a bouquet of white roses and purple-blue woods irises in one hand, her long veil caught up in the other. Her hair was loose. Shiny honey-gold waves swept past her shoulders.

Jonathan lifted the reins, and the buggy rolled forward to meet her at the edge of the walk.

She stopped at the fence and bent to unlatch the gate, but Jonathan leapt down and opened it for her. Her smile set his heart galloping. When he closed the gate behind her and offered his arm, the touch of her fingers through the sleeve of his summer frock coat sent a tremor through him.

She said nothing but climbed into the buggy and settled her skirts with an air of calm he envied. Regal as a fairy princess, she waited for him to join her on the tufted seat.

The mare started off with a jerk, and Jonathan swore under his breath. As Erika grabbed her bouquet, a small black book slipped from beneath the blooms and tumbled to the floor.

He retrieved it. The edges of the leather cover were rounded with use, and the volume fell open to the page marked by a worn purple ribbon. A Bible. The words were in German. He tucked it into her hand.

He tried to concentrate on guiding Daisy down Maple Street, remember to turn the corner at Chestnut and proceed toward the church, but he found his gaze pulled again and again to the small book she carried. He wondered what text she had chosen for today.

They were the last to arrive. A space had been left for his buggy in front of the steepled, white-painted structure, and Jonathan maneuvered the vehicle close to the street edge.

Erika had not spoken one single word. Now, as he helped her down, he voiced the only question that came to mind. "Is there anything you need before we go in?"

She met his gaze with unnerving candor. "Yes! Some brandy!"

"My thoughts exactly," he said without thinking. Before he could retract the words, she laughed, a low, musical trill of amusement bubbling out of her mouth. The sound cleared his brain and sent a rush of thankfulness through his consciousness.

A woman who can laugh on her wedding day. What a prize I've captured!

He resisted a sudden impulse to shout "Hallelujah." Then he remembered where he was on this scorching afternoon in September, recalled the circumstances leading up to this day and the events that would follow. It was not a laughing matter. His pervasive fear of failure hung over him like a pall.

"Come, Erika. We must be married before we can have the brandy."

"Then," she whispered as they turned toward the open church doors, "let us hurry!"

The entire population of Plum Creek crowded the wooden pews inside the small Methodist church. Erika kept her eyes on the simple altar, where Reverend Yard waited, but as she passed slowly down the aisle on Jonathan's arm, she heard gasps and a few whispers.

"Exquisite gown...I wonder where she...damned handsome woman...Doc's a lucky..."

Lydia Valey's four-year-old daughter convulsed the congregation by piping "Pretty lady!" at the top of her lungs.

Under her fingers, Erika felt the muscles of Jonathan's arm flex and relax. She tightened her hand. The net veil billowed behind her, tugging on her headpiece. She was glad of it. It reminded her she was earthbound, and that this afternoon, this wedding ceremony, was real and not something she was dreaming.

At the altar they stopped and stood in silence before the minister.

"Dearly beloved, we are gathered here together to join this man and this woman..."

Erika felt her body begin to tremble. Glancing down, she saw the lace outlining the low, square neckline of her dress flutter with each thudding beat of her heart. At the minister's request, she took Jonathan's offered hand.

His ice-cold fingers closed over hers. Good heavens, he was as frightened as she was!

She sneaked a surreptitious look at the tall man beside her. The softly looped silk ascot at his throat shuddered in rhythm with the pulsing vein visible beneath the tanned skin of his neck. *His heart, too, is pounding with apprehension at the step we are taking.* Her gaze moved to his jaw. A muscle worked as he clenched and unclenched his teeth.

"...and repeat after me. I, Jonathan Edward Callender..."

Jonathan's lips opened. "I, Jonathan Edward Callender, take thee, Erika Maria Scharffenberger..."

The minister blinked.

"Is correct, my name," Erika whispered.

"...to be my lawful wedded..."

She looked up at Jonathan, watching his mouth move as he repeated the vows. His eyes reminded her of the soft gray mist that sometimes rolled over the oat fields in Schleswig. He looked directly into her face, and suddenly she couldn't breathe.

His voice went on, low and steady, reciting the words that would bind them together for life. But his eyes shone with moisture.

Was he thinking of his dead wife? Remembering another wedding?

"...for richer or for poorer, in sickness and in health..."

When he finished, he did not return his gaze to Reverend Yard, but stood holding her hand in his, his beautiful, soft eyes searching hers. Erika's heart leapt, and a humming began inside her head.

His thoughts are not on Tess. He is thinking of me! Dear Lord in heaven, I shall surely die of joy!

From somewhere far away she heard a voice call her name.

"Erika? Erika, repeat after me." Reverend Yard waited until she acknowledged his request. She nodded and felt Jonathan's hand tighten on hers.

"I, Erika Maria Scharffenberger," she began. The rest was a blur. All she knew was that Jonathan looked straight into her eyes as she said the words, and sweet, lazy warmth crept from her toes to the crown of her head.

Jonathan saw Erika's dark blue eyes widen as Reverend Yard spoke her name a second time. It was time for her vows. He squeezed her hand as she began.

"...to have and to hold from this moment..."

Her clear, quiet voice carried the words to his brain and then straight into his heart. She pledged her life, her self, with such calm dignity he wondered at it. Earlier he'd thought she was frightened, or perhaps nervous. Now she spoke her wedding vows with quiet conviction.

"...for better or for worse...until death..."

His breath stopped. *Not death.* He willed himself not to let the word register, not to think about losing anyone, ever again. Especially not Erika.

Cold terror washed through his belly. He would watch over her, guard her, keep her from harm no matter what. Nothing must hurt or threaten her. She would be safe with him. She had to be.

"I now pronounce you man and wife." Reverend Yard smiled down at them.

"Dr. Callender, you may kiss your bride."

Chapter Fifteen

Jonathan cupped his hands around Erika's shoulders, felt her body heat through the thin sleeves of ivory silk. Her flesh shifted under his fingers, a delicate ripple of tissue over bone. She raised her face, her lashes fluttering closed, then opening again when he made no move. She tensed, waiting.

An expectant hush fell over the congregation. He took a single step closer to her and bent his head, brushing his mouth over hers. It was but a whisper of flesh touching flesh, but he felt it to the core of his being. She smelled of roses and warm sunshine, and when her breath wafted against his lips, his heart caught.

A pulse throbbed in her throat. An overwhelming, possessive joy swept through him. She was so alive! *And she was his!*

Deep inside he heard a silent voice cry out for

what she offered. Borne outside of himself on a surge of male instinct, he kissed her again, his senses inflamed, his lips hungry, insistent, imprinting the soft, tender mouth under his with his soul's desperate need.

Shaken, he stepped away from her and met her gaze. He expected shock, even outrage at his assault. Instead, her shadowed eyes held his in a look of recognition.

God in heaven, she was no simpering innocent, as Tess had been on their wedding day, but a woman full-blown, aware of herself. Aware of him.

An odd humming began in his brain, and in the same instant he became conscious of his heart slamming in irregular cadence against his ribs. He opened his mouth, and then Erika smiled at him.

My God, she is exquisite!

The thin wail of a child—his child, he realized dimly—pierced the quiet, and all at once the congregation came to life.

Reverend Yard leaned forward and spoke over the buzz of voices. "Congratulations, Dr. Callender, Mrs. Callender." He reached out a thin arm and gently turned Erika and Jonathan to face the pews.

People filled the aisle, surged toward them. Instinctively Jonathan secured Erika's hand on his arm and together they moved forward, through the crowd.

Erika tightened her fingers on the soft material of Jonathan's coat sleeve. It was done.

Her mind whirled with images—the minister's ruddy, beaming face, shiny with perspiration in the sweltering church. Mrs. Benbow dabbing her eyes with a white lace handerchief. The baby's cry, quieting now as Theodore Zabersky gently rocked the wicker carriage with one hand.

And Jonathan beside her, his heartbeat so strong she could feel it thudding against the back of her hand where it pressed his rib cage. She tightened her fingers on his arm.

At his side, she moved into the swirl of bodies, some sweaty, some perfumed, all pressing close to wish them well. Dazed, she clung to her husband, her thoughts still caught up in the kiss he had given her a few moments ago.

Oh, the memory of his mouth tentatively touching hers, then descending again with a questioning hot, sweet urgency... She would never forget it. Never.

Her body had felt warm and cold all over. Inside, something insistent, something glorious she had never experienced, began to unfurl.

Jonathan greeted the well-wishers, shook hands, spoke in low, measured tones, while Erika struggled to focus. Slowly he steered her through the throng toward the church door.

"Oh, my dear, you do look lovely!" Tithonia

Brumbaugh enfolded her in a bosomy embrace. "Why, you're shaking like a leaf! All brides are nervous, I know. I remember my own wedding day.... And Jon, you're shaking, too!"

"No doubt it's the heat, Tithonia," Jonathan replied.

"Now, come along, you two. The Presbyterian ladies have laid a lovely spread and there's to be dancing as well. Unlike the Methodists—" she cast a look of superiority at Reverend Yard "—we Presbyterians don't consider dancing a sin. Quite the contrary. Why, at my own wedding..."

Erika lost track of Tithonia's reminiscing as Jonathan drew her out the church door and down the single wooden step. "I am *not* shaking," he said in a low voice.

"Of course not," Erika agreed as they headed for the church hall across the street. But she knew the truth. His steps were as unsteady as hers, and underneath his black frock coat his heart pounded against his ribs. The knowledge brought her a strange sense of power. Whatever the reason, no matter how logical his protest, she knew that Jonathan Callender was affected by her.

When the crush of the receiving line on which Tithonia Brumbaugh had insisted began to ease, the first thing Erika became conscious of was Theodore Zabersky's violin. The lilting melody of "My Bonnie

Lies Over the Ocean" rose in the crowded room and
in an instant couples were swooping about the waxed
and polished plank floor.

Madison Lander lugged his accordion to the corner
where Mr. Zabersky stood, and soon another young
man joined them on his guitar. With surprise, Erika
recognized him from the Sunday-evening Methodist
services. Whitman Vahl. Whitman's fiancée, Mary
Zabersky, belonged to the Presbyterian quilting circle.

Jonathan tried to disengage his hand from the
grasp of the last guest through the line.

"I'm right glad for you," Rutherford Chilcoate
said, pumping the doctor's hand up and down once
more.

Jonathan wrenched his hand free, and to keep the
medicine vendor from capturing it again, slid it
around Erika's waist.

"Thank you, Rutherford."

"My pleasure, Doc. My very great pleasure." He
leaned forward and lowered his voice. "By the way,
you got anything stronger here than Mrs. B's Presbyterian punch? I see they don't mind dancin', but
serious drinkin' seems beyond the pale." He drifted
off to inspect the refreshment table, and suddenly
Erika found herself alone with her husband.

Tongue-tied, she gazed around the room. Tithonia
bounced in the arms of her husband as another waltz

floated on the warm late-afternoon air. The mayor's wife had a tendency to lead, Erika noted, but the mayor placidly allowed himself to be herded this way and that.

Plump Jane Munrow sat on the sidelines with Mary Zabersky, her stiff back pressed against the wall. Mary's young man, tall, rugged-looking logger Whitman Vahl, was absorbed in his guitar playing. Beside Mary, Susan Ransom squirmed in her peach sprigged muslin dress and expectantly eyed young Nate Ellis.

The tables groaned with pies and iced triple layer cakes. Mrs. Benbow bent over the assortment, a cake knife in one hand. A few yards away, Gwendolyn Shaunessey languidly rocked the baby carriage with one long, thin arm, a wistful look on her face as she watched the dancers.

"Are you hungry?" Jonathan asked.

The thought of food made Erika's stomach clench. "I— No, I could nothing eat."

"Would you like to dance, then?"

Dance! Move about on the floor with Jonathan's arms around her? She felt she might die of happiness.

"Oh, I, well, yes," she blurted. "Let us dance."

Jonathan bowed slightly and extended one hand. "Mrs. Callender?"

Dizzy with the heat in the crowded church hall, Erika hesitated. *Is this really me?* she wondered through a haze of joy. Plain Erika Scharffenberger, who sailed to a new country in the bowels of a ship and set off for the West with twenty dollars in her pocket? Who spoke no English but came anyway because she wanted to be an American?

Now she lived in Plum Creek, America, in a large, gracious house with many windows. She had never seen such windows—panes and panes of sparkling glass with lace curtains! And she was mama to a beautiful baby girl and... She caught her breath as her heart lifted under the tucked silk bodice.

And wife to Jonathan Callender. She resisted the urge to pinch herself.

Was it possible all this had really happened to her in a few short months? It seemed unreal, as if some kind of enchantment had been cast over her. She half believed she would waken at any moment and find herself back in Mrs. Benbow's kitchen, stirring cream into her tea.

"Mrs. Callender?" the man before her repeated. Eyes gray as a dove's wing sought hers. "Would you care to dance?"

Afraid to speak, Erika placed a trembling hand in Jonathan's and felt his warm fingers close over hers.

"It's a waltz, I believe."

Waltz? Polka? Schottische? It hardly mattered, so frozen were her feet in the buff-colored shoes. She felt like a fairy-tale princess, but her body refused to play its part. Slow and stiff, she moved in the circle of Jonathan's arms like a mechanical doll.

One, two, three...one, two, three... She concentrated on the forward-and-back pattern of steps as Jonathan guided her about the room. A half smile played on his lips, but his eyes, which never left her face, held a stillness Erika could not fathom. His expression did not change even when another couple inadvertently bumped into them. Jonathan took advantage of the nudge to draw her closer.

"Please," she whispered. "I warm easy."

Jonathan chuckled and eased his hand back to its original position.

The violin took up the strains of "Pop Goes the Weasel," and the dancers scrambled into a line for a reel. Jonathan led her off the floor, but he kept his arm protectively about her waist. She didn't mind that. It was the other, being held close to him, that made her head swim.

While the other guests clapped and stomped through the set, Erika wondered at her husband's serious demeanor. When the reel concluded, the accordion began a slow rendition of "Beautiful Dreamer," and Jonathan pulled her to him.

Caught close, she moved as if in a spell, conscious of his arm about her waist, his starched shirtfront brushing the tips of her breasts. Suddenly aware of the heat building in her belly, she backed away.

"What's wrong?" he murmured.

She felt her face and neck flush, knew her cheeks flamed. "N-nothing."

But something stirred inside her, and in that instant she recognized a growing unease. She was enclosed on all sides by the life she had accepted by becoming Jonathan Callender's wife. She was surrounded by the people of Plum Creek, by the four painted walls of the Presbyterian social hall, by the looks and knowing smiles of Tithonia Brumbaugh and the ladies of the quilting circle who eyed them with curious glances.

She was even surrounded by Jonathan! That thought triggered a new, even more disturbing one. *In a very real way, my life is no longer my own.*

Her husband's arm tightened. "Erika? What is it?"

"I like dance me loose," she whispered. "Otherwise, cannot breathe."

Instantly he widened the circle of his arms and drew away. "Better?" With a low chuckle, he watched her face.

Erika nodded. "Better, yes."

But still she could not breathe. Air pulled in and out of her lungs in uneven bursts, but try as she might, she could not control it. She felt she would suffocate with all these people encircling her, the hot, flower-scented air pressing in on her, the music pulsing in her brain. Her vision dimmed.

Jonathan caught her as she crumpled. Scooping her up in his arms, he strode toward the doorway, his bride's floor-length veil billowing behind him. Tithonia Brumbaugh's voice faded as he elbowed his way outside.

"I swooned myself at my wedding. You remember, don't you, Plotinus? You said how pale I looked and the next thing I knew..."

On the porch, Jonathan cradled Erika against his chest and gently blew a puff of air into her face. Her eyelids fluttered open.

"You fainted," he explained. "Don't be frightened, it's all right now."

She rested her head against his chin and drew in a shuddery breath. "First time," she whispered. "Never happen before. Was like dying!"

Jonathan watched her, hiding his relief. "Too much excitement, perhaps. Or too much hot air."

Erika choked back a laugh. "Is joke, correct? Americans very fond of 'hot air.' Missus Mayor, Dr. Chilcoate selling medicine—all hot air."

Jonathan laughed out loud. One thing was certain—while they might not live together as man and wife, with Erika Scharf as his partner, he was never going to be bored!

"Shall we return to the lion's den?" Amusement tinged his voice. "Or would you rather—"

"Yes, please!" Erika interjected. "I would rather some brandy."

Surprised and oddly pleased, Jonathan carried his new bride to the buggy waiting by the roadside. When he had settled her on the tufted leather seat, he retraced his steps inside to pay a quick visit to Tithonia, thanking her for the reception. Climbing aboard the buggy, he lifted the reins and snapped them over Daisy's neck. The wheels crunched as the vehicle lurched forward.

In silence they sat side by side in the wicker chairs he'd placed on the veranda, sipping generous dollops of brandy Jonathan had splashed into two china teacups. Twilight ebbed into dusk and then evening. Stars floated overhead like luminous diamonds, and in the deepening quiet, snatches of music and laughter floated from the Presbyterian church a block away.

The heat inside the house was still unbearable, Jonathan realized. When it was full dark, he went to the kitchen and cobbled together cold roast beef sandwiches for their supper, bringing them out to the veranda on a tray with tall glasses of chilled coffee. They ate with napkins spread over their laps to catch the crumbs.

Jonathan heard the grandfather clock strike ten. Mrs. Benbow appeared at the gate, bid good-night to Ted Zabersky and wheeled the baby carriage up the walk. Since they were shadowed on the south side of the wraparound porch, the housekeeper did not even glance in their direction but lifted the sleeping child out of the buggy and disappeared behind the front door screen. Her slow footsteps echoed until he heard the slap of the Dutch doors into the kitchen.

Jonathan had never known a woman to remain quiet as long as Erika did. The gossamer wedding veil bundled to one side, Erika sat unmoving while fireflies darted about the yard and crickets scraped in the darkness. After the sandwich and a second brandy, his nerves began to settle. He hadn't realized how tense he'd been until the muscles of his back and shoulders began to unknot.

The lights winked out in the upstairs windows at the Zaberskys' house next door. In the soft blackness Jonathan's attention was caught by the sound of breathing—Erika's and his own. Theirs was a curiously intimate sharing, he thought. So unlike being with Tess, who never ceased moving, gesticulating, talking.

This was different.

Erika was different.

He had done the right thing. He had chosen well. With no effort at all, he thought with an inward smile, he already heeded the admonition Reverend Yard had spoken during the wedding service. He honored the young woman who sat beside him.

What would follow from this night he could not begin to guess, but of one thing he was assured. He was glad Erika belonged to him, glad she would now be safe and protected in his household and in his life.

She stirred beside him, rose to her feet and gathered up the long veil in one hand. "I see to baby."

"Erika, wait. Mrs. Benbow can—"

"Mrs. Benbow not mama," she said quietly. "I am mama now."

Jonathan heard the pride in her voice, the little tremor as she spoke the simple words. *I am mama.*

She turned away from him and moved toward the front door. Inside the screen, she paused, a glimmer of ivory through the dark mesh.

"I thank you for everything, from bottom of my heart. I work hard, make good mama. Good wife."

Long after she had glided into the darkened interior of the house, Jonathan stared at the screen. With a twinge of conscience, he acknowledged at last what he had struggled with ever since he had laid eyes on Erika Scharf. Now more than ever, he wanted to follow Reverend Yard's additional wedding service directive. He longed to worship her body with his own.

God forgive him, but he wanted Erika as he'd

wanted no other woman—not even his deceased wife.

What in heaven's name had ever possessed him to propose a marriage in name only?

Chapter Sixteen

Erika patted the baby dry with a clean towel, dusted the silky pink skin with cornstarch and wrapped her in a light flannel blanket. "Now we are all clean," she crooned to the wriggling bundle. "And nice and cool for afternoon nap." After an hour in the stifling kitchen, she wished she could strip off her percale work dress and plunge into a tub of cool water as well.

How, she wondered, did Mrs. Benbow stand the oppressive heat in that black bombazine? To say nothing of drinking hot, hot tea on this scorching September day. At least the housekeeper lay down for a rest each afternoon, which was why Erika was alone in the kitchen at this moment. She lifted Marian Elizabeth onto her shoulder and pressed her nose against the baby's soft neck.

"Ah, my *Liebchen,* you smell sweet as a rose.

Come, we will sit in the parlor. Your papa has gone out to make someone well and will not be back until evening, so you and I, we will have the house to ourselves.''

She chatted on as she walked through the dining room, skirting the big walnut table where the supper place settings were already laid, and plopped down in the front parlor, next to the harp. She had a lesson with Mr. Zabersky in an hour, but it was too hot to practice.

In the two short weeks since her marriage to Jonathan Callender she had found little time to play her exercises and work on the arpeggios her teacher assigned each week. Being a doctor's wife brought a whole new set of challenges and things to learn. They had twice been invited for dinner in the homes of Plum Creek's leading citizens, and Erika knew that soon she faced being hostess at her own dinner party.

Her heart quailed at the prospect. She would have to make conversation in English! Wear one of the low-cut, overflounced silk gowns Mrs. Benbow had insisted she select from Bloomingdale's mail order catalog. Worse, she would have to stand next to Jonathan greeting guests and later bidding them goodnight. Being close to him sent her thoughts spinning.

In fact, she admitted, being anywhere near him made her heart sing and her body thrum with need.

She loved him. But she would not come to him until he needed her, too. Until he asked.

To cope with her wanting, she busied herself with the laundry, ironed the doctor's starched shirts, put up dozens of jars of thick plum jam, even dusted the upstairs rooms when the housekeeper's rheumatism prevented her from climbing the stairs. To those tasks she had lately added greeting the endless parade of patients who rang the front bell at all hours of the day and night and trooped in to consult the doctor about sore throats and dislocated shoulders and other, more private ailments.

Erika smiled in satisfaction. She was tired much of the time, but it was a good sort of fatigue. She was learning! Her elation at her progress made the daily burdens seem light. Even Mrs. Benbow expressed surprise at her accomplishments.

She was a good wife. In all ways but one.

Jonathan had said little these past two weeks. People came from as far as Gold Hill and Mill Creek City to seek the doctor's advice, and days passed when he was so busy with patients he missed both the noon meal and supper. She admired his dedication, his dogged perseverance in the face of what he described as "farm-family ignorance."

He worked hard. Too hard. Erika often found him seated at his desk, exhausted, his head in his hands and an untouched glass of brandy sitting at his elbow.

"Genug," she murmured, rocking Marian Elizabeth against her breast. More than enough. Jonathan was so busy being a physician he had no time to be a papa. "Not good for baby," she murmured.

She lifted her head as a rebellious thought crossed her mind. "Is not good," she repeated. And so it must change!

She would do just that, she resolved. Change things. She would start this very evening, the minute her husband walked in the door.

"Me!" Erika clenched her hands in her lap and stared at Mr. Zabersky. "You want me to—"

"Accompany the violin at the charity musicale," the professor finished for her. "Yes, my dear. On your harp."

"Oh, no. I could not possibly. I—I can play only chords, all broken up. Not real music. Not in front of people!"

Theodore Zabersky laid his weathered hand gently over her knotted fingers. "It is a simple song I have chosen. You have only to play your chords, 'all broken up,' to keep me company."

Erika looked away from the old man's expectant face. "Why not your daughter Mary," Erika pleaded. "Piano sounds beautiful when at night I listen through the window."

The professor shook his head. "Mary has outgrown me. She is playing a duet with her intended, Mr. Vahl.''

Whitman Vahl, Erika remembered, had played reels and waltzes at her wedding reception two weeks ago. ''He plays only guitar, is that it? Is an instrument for dancing.''

''Exactly.'' Mr. Zabersky coughed and cleared his throat. ''You can imagine my distress at Mary's choice of…partner.''

Aghast, Erika stared at him. It had never occurred to her Mr. Zabersky did not approve of his daughter's engagement. ''You can forbid?''

''Ah, no. This is America,'' he reminded her.

Erika was silent. *America.* There was a price for freedom in her new country, she was learning. The Indians, occupants of the land before the settlers came, were no longer allowed to live on their ancestors' land. Instead, they were shunned, sent to reservations. And, she knew from her own experience, those who protested an Indian's treatment were misunderstood. Or worse.

And there were other things that puzzled her. In America daughters could marry whom they wished, even if it made the papas unhappy, yet wives were still expected to obey husbands? It made no sense.

Her insides clenched. At this very moment she was planning a very unwifelike rebellion.

What had happened to her these past weeks? Ever

since she had pledged her life as Jonathan Callender's wife, she'd felt different. Elevated in social status, of course, but that mattered little to her. More important, she was accepted, her company sought out at church and on social occasions. She was becoming one of them. An American.

And yet...there was more. It was as if she had in some way grown larger inside the confines of her corset stays and the soft challis wrappers and walking gowns she now wore in addition to her serviceable navy work skirt and white waists. Larger and at the same time more *herself*.

And that brought its own obligation. Suddenly she knew she had to perform with Mr. Zabersky at the musicale. She wanted to prove herself, be accepted on her own merits, not simply because she was the respected Dr. Callender's wife.

I am my own person, she thought. She was a free woman in a free country. Only now was she beginning to realize what obligations that envied state carried. She must try all her life to be two persons—Mrs. Dr. Callender and herself, plain Erika Scharffenberger.

"Yes," she announced to her music teacher. "I will do it."

Jonathan fought to keep his eyes open. The buggy bounced along the town road, hardened by a sum-

mer's relentless sun and rutted by three generations
of horses, wagons and leather boot heels. He'd come
from the Ellis place, where eleven-year-old Timmy
complained of leg cramps. When Martha Ellis described her son's other symptoms—diarrhea and co-
pious vomiting—Jonathan's heart sank.

Cholera. The Ellises drew their water directly from
the polluted creek.

He flapped the reins, urging the tired mare home
at a faster pace. After instructing Martha in the only
possible treatment for her sick son—large amounts
of boiled water to offset dehydration—he'd made the
rounds of all the outlying farms along the creek and
the Devitt and Rukavin spreads in the surrounding
valley, as well. "Boil your drinking water and scrub
your hands," he'd ordered.

Everyone had scoffed at him but Abe Rukavin.
Abe had listened attentively. "We will do," the
rangy farmer had promised.

Jonathan would visit the Ellis boy again in the
morning, but now there was work to be done. Rutherford Chilcoate had agreed to rent him the warehouse next to the bank, and Jonathan intended to turn
the building into a hospital. With any luck at all, he
could get it cleaned and organized before an epidemic struck the town.

He grabbed the whip from its socket and flicked
it over Daisy's head, something he rarely did. He'd

have to scrub and disinfect the plank floor and dusty walls, round up some cots and clean bedding. If he worked hard all night, his hospital could be ready by sunup.

By the time he reined up in front of his house, he wondered if he had the strength to disembark, let alone work efficiently.

The front door stood open to catch what evening breeze there might be. Jonathan sat staring at it for a long minute before he gathered up his black medical bag and his jacket, discarded earlier as he made his rounds. He plodded through the gate and up the porch steps.

The sound of Erika's harp floated through the screen door. For a moment he stood rooted, drinking in the silvery notes and fighting off the hunger he always felt when he came near her. One night when he'd been unable to sleep, he'd stumbled on her in the library, poring over her dictionary. At the sight of her unbound hair, her small bare toes peeking beneath the blue nightrobe, he'd been unable to speak. He felt the same way now as the music washed over him.

He let the screen slam shut behind him, masking his desire with anger in a way he only half understood. He relished the startled cry that came from the front parlor. A baby's wail followed, and Jonathan groaned. The last thing he needed was a squalling infant.

Erika took one look at him and rose to her feet. "Have you eaten?"

"Haven't had time. Wake Mrs. Benbow, would you? Tell her I need a lantern and a bucket and a scrub brush. And hot water—lots of it."

She sent him an assessing look, picked up the baby and thrust her into his arms. "Watch baby. I will heat water." She swished past him.

He stared at the blanketed lump in his arms. "Erika!"

She halted in the doorway.

"Take the baby. I'll get the water."

"No. Baby needs papa sometimes. Rock her. Maybe sing to her."

"Sing! I don't have time to—"

"You have time for bucket and water," she snapped. "You have time for baby. Baby needs to be with you. Besides," she added, raising one eyebrow in a challenging look, "*you* need it!" She pronounced the words with deliberate care, then marched into the hall.

Dumbstruck, Jonathan stared after her. She acted for all the world like a wife of twenty years! Where was the quiet, serene creature he'd wed?

The baby wriggled and began to scream. In desperation, he laid the thrashing body against his chest and began to hum. By the time he'd finished the second verse of "Rock of Ages," Erika reappeared, a work apron tied over her muslin dress, a tin bucket in each hand. "Take baby to Mrs. Benbow and bring the teakettle and the lantern by the door. I will help."

"You! Erika, you needn't—"

"I need," she said quietly. "You are tired, hungry. I bring sandwiches. Two can work faster than one."

"Don't you want to change your dress? It's a filthy warehouse. I've got to get it clean, set up an infirmary, but you—"

"In-firm-ary," she repeated. He half expected her to set the buckets down and pull a notepad and pencil from her apron pocket.

"It's a kind of hospital."

She nodded, and without another word moved to the front door.

"Erika, I—" His throat closed over the words. Gratitude and something else—pride—brought tears stinging into his eyes.

"Come," she said. "If we do not hurry, you will miss your breakfast, too."

Side by side they worked all night scrubbing lye soap over the splintery planks of the rough pine floor. By dawn the place was clean and aired out, the windows washed until they sparkled, the six cots loaned by the Methodist church set up and in place. Too tired to talk, they made up the beds together. Jonathan made neat army corners in the sheets. Erika snapped the folds square the way her mother had taught her.

When the last blanket lay folded in place at the foot of each bed, Erika faced him with a tired but triumphant smile. "Is ready."

She arched her back, rubbed her palms against her aching muscles. Her skirt was filthy with cobwebs and dust, the front splotched with scrub water. She'd unbuttoned her shirtwaist to the throat and rolled up the sleeves, revealing red, water-shriveled hands. Hair straggled from her once-tidy braids.

Jonathan stared at her. Dirty and disheveled as she was, she had never been more appealing. With difficulty he kept himself from pulling her into his arms.

Later. Later he would tell her how beautiful she was at this moment, tell her of his growing feelings for her.

She moved toward him, lifted his hand from the bucket handle. "Let us go home, eat breakfast." Stretching on tiptoe, she brushed her lips against his stubble-rough cheek.

"You are good man, Jonathan," she whispered. "Good doctor, also. And soon..." She stepped back and lifted her gaze to meet his. "Soon you will be good papa, too."

She sent him a smile that dazzled his heart with its warmth.

But as they walked together out of the new warehouse-hospital and climbed wearily into the waiting buggy, Jonathan noted what she had *not* said, and an odd twinge of regret tugged at him.

She had said nothing at all about his being a good husband.

Chapter Seventeen

For three days the young Ellis boy struggled for life against the disease ravaging his body. Jonathan sat at his bedside for hours, dribbling boiled salt water into his parched mouth with a teaspoon. *Dear God, he's not yet twelve years old! Let him live, Lord. Please, let him live!*

Then the Devitt family took sick. All five of them drove into town in their wagon to enter Jonathan's hospital. When the remaining infirmary bed was filled, Jonathan knew it was the beginning of the epidemic he had feared.

More cots came, this time from the Presbyterians, and Gwendolyn Shaunessey defied her aging mother and came to help nurse. Jonathan told Erika she must stay away, fearing she would catch the highly contagious disease. To protect the baby, Erika complied.

Every evening he scrubbed his hands and arms

before he walked the three blocks to his home. And each night he gobbled the sandwiches or the bowl of soup Erika or Mrs. Benbow left for him, then lay awake agonizing about his treatment of the burgeoning number of patients who had contracted the fever.

Old Mrs. Eubanks succumbed. Then two of the Devitt children, aged six and nine. Mrs. Devitt was too sick to realize the loss, but Adam, their father, stood beside Jonathan at the two small graves and wept in hoarse, racking sobs.

The following morning, dehydration and grief took Mrs. Devitt as well, despite Jonathan's desperate efforts to save her by forcing salted water down her throat. At the end, she couldn't swallow.

Sick at heart, he fought the pull of exhaustion and despair. Once a person contracted cholera, he could do little to save them, and the fact that the outbreak could have been prevented had the townspeople heeded his warnings early in the summer added to the helpless rage burning inside him. He drank more brandy than he knew was prudent, and he longed for Erika beside him through the long night hours.

Occasionally he heard the harp as she practiced for the charity musicale. It seemed the only ordered, beautiful element in a nightmare of illness and disillusion.

The night he lost Timmy Ellis was the worst. In

despair, Jonathan left the hospital and stumbled home, his eyes unseeing.

Erika was sitting on the cool veranda, fanning herself with a broom twist. When she saw him, she rose and came down the steps toward him.

"You look dreadful, Jonathan! What is wrong?"

"Timmy Ellis died." He wrapped his arms about her, leaned his forehead against her crown of braids. "I couldn't save him." His voice broke, and he stopped to regain control. "I did everything I could think of, but it wasn't enough!"

Erika's arms slid around him. "Is not your fault, Jon. You tried your best. Others you have saved, many others. Think of them."

"I can't. Oh, Erika, I don't know what to believe in anymore, God or medicine or—"

But he did believe in one thing, he realized. He believed in Erika. His wife.

She held him, saying nothing, and then she turned toward the house. Taking his hand, she led him up the steps and through the door.

The familiar smell of the house comforted him. Lemon oil, fragrant white roses in a crystal bowl, freshly baked bread. He stopped abruptly in the main hall and pulled a life-sustaining breath into his lungs.

"Erika. Erika! I don't want to be alone tonight."

He hadn't realized he'd spoken aloud until Erika

raised her arm and gently rested her hand against his cheek.

"Yes," she said, her voice quiet. "Is time. After baby sleeps."

Jonathan's heart leapt. Had he heard right, or was he merely hallucinating? Erika would be with him tonight? His heart beat so raggedly, he could barely voice the question. *Did she mean as his wife?*

Erika insisted he have a warm bath to calm his nerves. She set about heating three full teakettles of water, poured them into the copper tub on the laundry porch, and dropped in sprigs of rosemary to scent the water. He was too tired to question her presence as he pulled off his trousers and rumpled shirt and stepped into the vessel.

Sinking into the soothing water, he closed his eyes and listened to her footsteps as she moved about the porch. He sat unmoving for a solid hour, soaking away the ache in his heart, wondering what her words had meant. Something different was happening between them. He had sensed it ever since the night they had scrubbed down the hospital together.

When he opened his eyes, his garments had disappeared and in their place lay a clean nightshirt and his lounging robe. When she bustled into the kitchen, he dried himself off. Ignoring the nightshirt, which he never wore, he shrugged into the robe.

Erika had warmed up the stew Mrs. Benbow had

made for supper and poured out a glass of cool milk from the pantry. "Eat," she ordered when he appeared. "Mrs. Benbow watch over baby tonight. I watch over you."

The lump in his throat dissolved, and Jonathan clenched his fingers on the edge of a straight-backed kitchen chair.

Maybe there was some meaning in life. At least there was order and caring here in his own household. He was too tired and heartsick to think beyond this moment. All he wanted was to assuage the hunger of his soul through the long night ahead of him. All he wanted was to hold Erika in his arms and forget everything else.

Erika drew the light cambric gown over her head, blew out the lamp and closed the door of her small bedroom behind her. On quiet feet she moved down the hall to Jonathan's room, entered and pulled the door shut. She paused to let her eyes adjust to the dark.

Why am I not frightened, or nervous? she wondered. She was neither, even though this would be her first time with a man. She didn't know how it would be, whether she would like it or not. All she knew was that she wanted to be near him, her body touching his, had wanted it for a long time now but had held back until it felt right.

Tonight it felt right. Tonight he needed her, not only as one human being needs another, but as a man needs a woman. She didn't know how she knew this, she just did. Witch-vision, her mother used to say. Whatever it was, Erika had never been more sure of anything in her life.

"Erika?"

Her heart caught. His voice sounded near, drowsy with need.

"Yes?"

A shadow moved toward her in the dark. "Erika, I..."

She waited, afraid to move.

"I know how a man is, with a woman, I mean," he said at last. "What I don't know is how Jonathan is to be with Erika."

"I, too, do not know," she said in a low voice.

"I feel unsure of myself. I don't want to hurt you. Or...disappoint you."

Erika released a pent-up breath. "Perhaps you will not do either."

He gave a tired laugh. "Perhaps I will do both."

"Is not possible, I think." Then she added in a small voice, "Is it?"

Jonathan chuckled again and reached for her in the dark. "I do not know, my darling Erika. And what is more..." He gathered her unbound hair in his hands, buried his face in it. "I do not care. By morning it will not matter."

Erika opened her lips to reply, but found his mouth instead. After a long, heart-stopping minute, she found it already did not matter.

He knew she was untouched. He could tell by her hesitant response to his mouth and hands. Her breathing grew uneven as he deepened the kiss, and at last she broke away and clung to him, turning her face to his chest.

"I have not much practice in kissing," she whispered. "In Schleswig, mostly I read books with Papa at night."

Her confession surprised him. Someone as vibrant as Erika, with eyes as clear and blue as a midsummer sky and hair the color of honey, must have captured the heart of every male who laid eyes on her. "Were there no young men in your village?"

"Oh, yes, but I am not allowed. And not see young men at my school. My school is separate, for girls. After school, I study with Papa. Mama, too, until...until she died."

Jonathan smiled into her hair. That explained many things about his unusual wife. He'd bet she was better educated than any woman in Plum Creek.

He tipped her chin up with his forefinger. "You are a remarkable woman, Erika. So wise in unexpected ways, yet so young, really." He cupped her face and stroked his thumbs along the line of her chin.

"I am twenty and four."

"I am thirty and seven," he responded softly. "And I, too, studied with my father when I was young." He pressed his mouth against her temple. "He taught me one thing I had forgotten until this moment."

He heard her suck in her breath as he moved his lips to her cheekbone. Her eyes were closed, her body trembling as he continued his kisses, bringing his mouth closer and closer to hers.

"What...what was it you forgot?"

"I had forgotten how sweet it is to kiss a woman, just kiss her and not have to say anything."

She lifted her face. "Your papa taught you this?"

"My father, yes." He grazed her lips with his thumb. "And my mother. I used to watch them together. They seemed to communicate without talking."

"And did they kiss?" she asked shyly.

"Yes. That's how they communicated. Like this." He bent his head and covered her upturned mouth. Deliberately moving his lips over hers, he tasted the sweetness of her small, wet tongue, and a humming began in his brain.

"You can say anything to me, Erika," he said against her still-open lips. "Anything you wish." He grasped her hands, lifted both her arms about his neck. "Or you can show me what you feel. What you want, without talking."

"I want you should kiss me more," she breathed.

Jonathan chuckled. "Kiss me more, but dance me loose, is it?"

"Yes," she said with a soft laugh. "But kiss me tight."

Jonathan's heart stuttered. She wanted him. She might not recognize it yet, but her words and her unguarded physical response to him told him more than could be expressed in mere words. She was like a flame, a glimmer of passion flickering just beneath the surface. Before this night was over, he resolved, she would burn hot and fierce, and he would be the instrument of her most secret desires.

The thought made him hard. He kissed her again, moved both hands to the buttons at the neck of her gown. He slipped the first one free and heard her moan under his mouth.

He blew his warm breath into the hollow of her throat, slowly working the remaining buttons. Her arms tightened around his neck, and then he felt her fingers in his hair. Her hands...he wanted her hands on his skin.

Gently he turned her face away and breathed softly into the shell of her ear. She gasped and then shuddered. He parted the unbuttoned gown and slipped his hands inside, cupping her breasts.

Erika whimpered with pleasure. "Oh," she whispered, and then, "Oh, yes. Yes."

Without speaking, he stepped out of his silk robe. He had nothing on underneath.

"Touch me," he said.

She laid her palm lightly against his shoulder, then let it slide to his bare chest. When he kissed her, she brought her other hand up and smoothed the skin over his breastbone. At her touch, he began to tremble inside.

Her mouth opened under his, inviting, tentatively exploring. And then she lowered her arms and her night robe slid down and came away in his hands. Silken and warm, she pressed against him.

He lifted her, bent to kiss her neck as she curled her body against him. Her head fell back as he caressed her small, perfect breasts.

He moved then to the large double bed and lowered her to the sheet. It was cool in his room. The paned windows on two adjoining walls were propped wide open, and a honeysuckle-scented breeze wafted over them. He drew in a lungful of the soft late-summer air and forced himself to proceed slowly.

Erika gazed up at the man standing over her and felt herself float as if borne up on wings. Her heart fluttered irregularly, and her breasts ached for Jonathan's hands, his mouth, once more. She arched toward him.

He knelt over her, ran his palms up her sides and across her ribs and then down over her belly. Between her thighs he stroked one finger up, then up again, higher this time, so that his knuckles brushed the hair at the apex. She shivered with pleasure, then gasped and went perfectly still as he touched her. Instinctively she raised her hips, hungry for more.

With a low, satisfied laugh, Jonathan kissed her. "Show me, Erika," he whispered against her lips. "Tell me what you want."

She moved his hand to her thigh again. "This."

Chuckling, Jonathan trailed his fingers up her thigh, but he waited until she began moving with him before moving deeper. When he did, she jerked and halted her motions. And then she gave a small, soft laugh.

"Is wonderful, is it not? So fine. So shaky inside."

"It is," Jonathan said. He kissed her breast, swirled his tongue around her nipple, and she began to breathe in soft pants.

As he drew his kisses lower, Erika moaned, and her breathing grew more ragged. She reached for him, twisted his hair in her fingers, wanted him never to stop. A ripple of pleasure began low in her belly, pulsed again and then again through her center, and she cried out.

Jonathan rose over her. He positioned his body, and she reached for him, pulling him down to her. He entered her quickly, and there was a short, sharp pain and then fullness. He moved inside her, and the pleasure began again.

And then deep, deep inside her he touched something and she exploded.

Jonathan shouted when the spasms came, wrenching her, driving her beyond herself. She heard her own voice cry out, and when it was over she clung to him and wept as his guttural breathing slowed.

He did not withdraw, but held her, rocking slowly back and forth, his hands under her hips. She convulsed again, waves of sensation tightening into a burst of feeling, and Jonathan laughed a contented laugh.

"As your physician, Mrs. Callender, I'd say you are a very passionate woman."

Erika brushed her wet cheeks and smiled up at him.

"But as your husband..." He caught her hand, brought it first to his lips and then placed it where their bodies were still joined. "As your husband, I'd say you are now my very married wife."

Before she could answer, he began again to rock his body with hers, and in a few moments Erika forgot everything but the flowering of her pleasure with his.

Chapter Eighteen

Afraid she would break into a skip before she reached the kitchen, Erika forced her feet to a sedate pace as she descended the stairs. She could fly! She could sing! She could eat a dozen of Mrs. Benbow's buckwheat pancakes and scrub three loads of laundry!

Never had a night passed so quickly. Or so pleasurably! She pressed her hands to her hot cheeks, then ran her tongue over her kiss-swollen lips. She had never known passion until last night. Love she had known—love of Mama and Papa. And love of Jonathan ever since that day in the garden.

But not like this. This love was sweet and urgent and freeing.

Passionate, he had said she was. His voice had shaken when he had spoken the words.

She pushed through the Dutch doors into the

kitchen. Though the sun had barely risen, the interior of the room was already hot, and a delicious cinnamony smell hung in the air. Mrs. Benbow looked up from the stove where she was arranging a batch of freshly baked tarts on a serving platter.

"For tea," the housekeeper said. "Ted—Mr. Zabersky comes for your lesson today." She cast an assessing gaze on Erika and stifled a smile.

"Hungry, are ye? You look positively radiant, my girl, so I expect you're near starvin', as well. Always thought it odd that lovin' and eatin' went together, but…"

Her voice trailed off as Erika threw her arms around her and hugged her tight. "Thank you, Mrs. Benbow. I'll just get my apron and wash up for you. Then I'll feed the baby and practice my chords before the professor comes."

"Baby's fed already and napping in the parlor. You practice first, lass. Tithonia's musicale is in two weeks."

Erika froze with her hands on the apron ties. *Two weeks?* So soon? She wasn't ready! She would never be ready!

Panic chased away her euphoria. "It's to be held at Mrs. Brumbaugh's? Oh, I can't!"

The housekeeper eyed her. "Now, there's a word I haven't heard you use before—'can't.' Why ever can't you?"

"Because it's Tithonia," Erika blurted. "And the Presbyterian ladies, the quilting circle ladies, will be there, watching me. Waiting for me to make a mistake in the English or...or proper behavior. I do not know enough."

Mrs. Benbow paused, the pastry spatula in her uplifted hand. "Sure enough they'll be there, along with everybody else in town. This is a big money-raising event for Plum Creek public projects, and everyone who lives here in the valley will be there!"

Erika caught her lower lip between her teeth. "I want Jon—Dr. Callender to be proud of me. Be glad he married me."

"He's glad, lass," the housekeeper replied with a chuckle in her voice. "Should'a seen him this morning. Sang all the way out to the barn to feed the mare, he did. 'Beautiful Dreamer,' it was. Seems to me *glad* is more important than *proud*. He's already had *proud*. And I don't mind sayin' it wasn't enough. There, now, I've gone and scorched the porridge!"

Erika watched the older woman duck her head and turn toward the stove. *"Glad" is better than "proud"?*

But there was more to it than Jonathan's approval of her. She wanted to prove her worth, wanted to be proud of herself, *for herself.*

That, she admitted, was why she was frightened.

More frightened than she'd been since the day she stepped off the boat in New York's busy harbor.

Theodore Zabersky showed up on the stroke of four, bent over Mrs. Benbow's hand with a gallantry Erika hadn't seen since she left the old country, and started her lesson ten minutes late because his conversational pleasantries kept the housekeeper talking.

Erika's nerves were on edge. Halfway through her arpeggios, her hands shook so violently she had to stop.

"Never mind, my dear," the professor offered, his manner unruffled. "I have brought my violin—we will try it again, together." He unsnapped the black instrument case and lifted out his Eichheimer.

"Now we play it again, from the beginning."

Erika gritted her teeth and tried to concentrate. C major, then G major, then A minor...

It went badly, and at the end of the hour Erika excused herself from tea and fled to her room, leaving Mrs. Benbow to serve the cinnamon tarts.

She must think! Must get her emotions under control. She thought it strange—laughable, even—that the specter of Tithonia's disapproval loomed larger than Jonathan's. After all, he was her husband! Worse, Erika's own approval of herself mattered more than even Tithonia's!

"But, why?" she muttered. "Why should that be

true?'' She folded her arms on the windowsill and rested her head against them. *Why?*

Because, a voice inside her said, *you want to belong. To be accepted.* Jonathan already accepted her, and he'd shown that last night. Besides, his acceptance was based on things between husband and wife. Between a man and a woman.

How odd it was that she felt more confident today as a woman than as a member of Plum Creek society. As an American. It seemed illogical, but it was true. More than anything else, she wanted to belong, to count in Plum Creek. She wanted it because she believed in the things America stood for—equality and justice. Freedom for everyone.

Yet what did Tithonia Brumbaugh's charity musicale have to do with these things?

Nothing, she reasoned. And everything. It was the residents of Plum Creek—women—who arranged nursing shifts at Jonathan's infirmary, supported the school, hemmed blankets for the poor, organized social relief projects. It was women who made a difference in how the town grew. At this very moment they were raising money for Jonathan's hospital and for his new water system. She wanted to be part of it. She wanted her life to *count.*

"Oh, God forgive me," she moaned. "I do also want to please Jonathan."

And so you shall, spoke the voice. *But you must*

be yourself. In order to please him, you must please yourself.

"Why could it not be easier?" she asked aloud. "Other women pretend. They all the time put on false fronts. Why not me?"

Because you are not other women. You are you.

"Very well," she said at last. "I am me, plain Erika Scharffenberger, from little village in Schleswig."

She lifted her head. "I try my best."

Three more residents of Plum Creek died from the ravages of cholera before Jonathan sensed the epidemic had peaked. In all, twenty-one people had succumbed over the past two weeks. Erika wept each time he brought home news of another loss.

Now everyone in town and on the surrounding farms boiled their water and moved their privies away from the creek. If only they'd listened to him sooner! If they had paid attention, the two Devitt children and Timmy Ellis would be alive to start school again next month. And Gwen Shaunessey and young Susan Ransom, who served as volunteer nurses, wouldn't look gaunt and tired. Gwen in particular. Already too thin, the widow looked as if she would blow away in a stiff breeze, and two spots of high color marked her slack cheeks. Twice Jonathan had ordered her home to rest, but she had reappeared the following morning, donned her starched nurse's apron and followed him down the row of cots, notepad in hand, as she did now.

He often wondered at Gwen's devotion to duty, then remembered he had once courted her, before he had married Tess. The widow would not have made him a good wife; she was too set in her preferences. Besides, he discovered he hadn't a spark of affection for her other than as a friend.

But she made a superb nurse. Slowly he made his evening rounds to check on the hospital patients, Gwen at his elbow. After a day on horseback calling on families in the valley, his back muscles were stiff and his head ached.

The Ransom girl, too, worked long hours on little sleep, taking for granted her apparently limitless energy and recuperative power. Jonathan groaned inwardly. Youth was indeed wasted on the young.

His thoughts strayed to Erika. She was his wife now in body as well as name. She, too, appeared to have an abundance of vitality, undiminished by successive nights of lovemaking. He stumbled over a china chamber pot thinking of it, regained his balance by grabbing the curtain of sheeting separating the infirmary beds.

Plotinus Brumbaugh had helped erect the privacy barriers. Tithonia had disapproved of the ward arrangement and had stitched up the drapes with the help of Jane Munrow and the Presbyterian ladies' aid society. Odd, how people reacted in a crisis.

Tithonia had been furious at him all summer for harassing her husband and the rest of the town council about the existing unsanitary water system. But when her niece, Ardith, fell ill and almost died from the bacillus he'd warned them about, Tithonia had proposed the charity musicale to raise money to finance the water project.

The town would have a real hospital! Brumbaugh Memorial it would be called if, as Jonathan suspected, Plotinus and his wife contributed a goodly share of the costs from their own pocket. He thought the matter over as he dictated instructions to Gwen.

"More salted water tonight for the Ottesen boy. And sponge down Mrs. Linderholm about every hour. I believe her fever will break by morning."

He moved on, touching hands, chests, foreheads, talking over his shoulder. All the while, like a cool river flowing at the back of his mind, thoughts of Erika rose to fill him.

He remembered the day he'd yanked open the front door and found her on the veranda with her dark blue eyes widening in wonder, her lips twisting over the English words. He recalled how she had stood up to him, fisting her small, capable hands on her hips, when he'd discovered the goat.

And he thought of their first time together just a

couple of weeks ago. She was his now. His wife. His property, in effect. Always and forever.

Or was she? Unbidden, other images rose. Erika closeted in the front parlor for her harp lesson with Ted Zabersky. Erika in a new blue sateen afternoon dress, bustling out the front door to attend the ladies' aid meeting, or help at the Methodist pie social, or...a hundred things.

"No food for Mr. Lander until tomorrow. Ice chips only."

"Yes, Doctor."

He moved to the next bed, felt for the thin wrist of eleven-year-old Sally Sinclair, who gazed up at him with adoring brown eyes.

"I'm going to get well, aren't I, Dr. Callender? I just know it! I have a new pony, and a new dress with puffed sleeves! I'm hungry, and I want something new to read!"

Jonathan smoothed her wiry red hair and suddenly thought of his baby daughter. In a few short years she, like Sally, would be eager for ruffled dresses and leather-bound books.

He straightened, but instead of moving on to the last bed, he stood rooted, remembering that day two weeks ago when Erika had thrust his baby daughter into his arms. He'd handled hundreds of infants, had delivered them, sponged them off, held them while their mothers were bathed and their gowns and bedding changed. Yet when his own child, Marian Elizabeth—named after his mother, he now recalled—had been plopped against his chest, his heart had all but stopped beating with pure, unvarnished fear. He could not fathom why.

A glimmer of insight made him catch his breath. He felt like a stranger in his own household. An outsider. The land, the structure he'd built on it belonged to him. He'd known Mrs. Benbow since he was a youth, had paid her salary to keep house for him for the past seventeen years. He'd married Erika, made her his in physical fact, and yet...

And yet when he tramped home from the hospital each night, entered the serene, ordered world that Erika had managed to create in the few months since she'd come, he felt left out in some way, as if he didn't belong there. He had created the family unit—father, mother, child—but *he* seemed to be missing.

He was alienated, he realized suddenly. From his child. From himself. Only with Erika beside him at night did he know himself, understand what he believed in.

But who are you, inside? What manner of man?

He had never asked such questions of himself when Tess was alive. Why had he stumbled into the abyss now, when his heart was full at last, his life blessed?

"Dr. Callender? Are you all right?"

"What?" He gave the nurse a quick nod. "Oh. Of course."

But he was not, he reflected as he adjusted his stethoscope and bent over the last patient. He was missing something. Something important.

The heartbeat underneath the metal chest piece echoed in his ears with satisfying regularity. "You're as healthy now as the day you were born, Rutherford. But when you go home tomorrow, I want you to drink lots of water—boiled, naturally. And stay away from spirits."

"Sure, Doc. Thanks."

"And not one drop of that elixir!"

The medicine hawker nodded. "Maybe I'll hafta change the recipe a bit."

Jonathan clapped his shoulder. He'd saved the man's life, and the lives of scores of others, as well. He was successful at the profession he loved—medicine. He was respected. He'd made a good life in Plum Creek. What could possibly be missing?

Once more he recalled his feelings when Erika had placed his daughter in his arms. Along with pure, heart-stopping fear, he'd felt off balance. Afraid he would fail. Afraid he would lose something precious to him.

Had he separated himself from his own flesh and blood to protect himself? Was he allowing himself to be estranged from his daughter because he himself had purposely stepped away from her? If that were true, it was only a matter of time before he would distance himself from Erika, as well.

He didn't want to. But human beings were what they were, and as a physician he knew that in his anxiety he would bring about the very thing he feared. Loss.

For the past month he'd watched children die of cholera, ached at their agony, wept with their parents at gravesites. And all the while he believed such a tragedy would not touch him because...

Because he had not allowed himself to love his child.

Erika had seen it all along. That day she handed Marian Elizabeth over to him, a crack had appeared in the wall.

Blind instinct drove his feet down the length of the infirmary to the doorway. He had to see Erika, had to tell her.

"I'm going home for an hour," he announced.

Without waiting for a reply, he began to walk, then to run, toward the big gray house on Maple Street.

Mrs. Benbow clutched at his sleeve the instant she saw him. "Why, whatever is the matter?" she croaked. "Is it Erika? Has something happened?"

"Adeline, where is she?"

"At the Brumbaughs'. Tonight's the musicale.

Lordy, from the look on your face I thought— You'll have to hurry, or you'll be late. I've laid out your clean shirt, and…''

Tithonia's musicale! He'd completely forgotten about it. A twinge of unease escalated into inexplicable anger.

Erika was out, occupied with something that didn't involve him. She was his wife, and she had a life separate from his. Separate from him!

He raced upstairs to bathe and change. He didn't want Erika to be separate. He wanted her all to himself. It was selfish, perhaps, but the truth. He needed her. She had a child, a husband, a household to run, social standing in the community. What more did a woman—even a woman as unusual as Erika—need?

With an odd sense of foreboding, he tore off his day shirt and trousers, scrubbed his hands and sponge-bathed the rest of his torso in the basin on his dresser. Then he dressed hurriedly for the evening event.

Before he left the house, something propelled him into the nursery where his daughter lay sleeping. He tiptoed in and for a long minute stared down at the child. Her tiny fingers were curled into a fist outside the pink-and-white quilt.

A choking feeling of awe swept over him. His throat constricted, aching as an apple-sized lump lodged in it. He felt happier and at the same time more frightened than ever before in his life.

He was so close, *so close,* to finding happiness at last. To finding himself. He couldn't let it slip through his fingers a second time. He couldn't bear it.

Erika. Erika! He would fight to keep her. He would do anything—*anything*—to keep Erika safe in his house, and in his heart.

And he would try, no, he would succeed! He would learn to be a papa.

Chapter Nineteen

Dozens of candelabra glowed with light in the Brumbaughs' oversize front parlor. Jonathan was grateful the guests were already seated, their backs to him, when he arrived. His hands had shaken so much he hadn't managed to fasten all his shirt studs. In his haste, he'd stuffed the last two in his watch pocket and hoped no one would notice.

He had to see Erika, had to hold her, tell her how much she meant to him, how frightened he was of losing her.

Too late, he realized as he scanned the room. Every chair was filled, and the performers for the evening were closeted somewhere out of sight. The recital had started.

Jonathan eased into a shadowed corner as a trio of women assembled in front of the ornately carved square grand piano and began to sing "Ave Maria," accompanied by Jane Munrow. Jane made a number of mistakes, but finally the trio warbled to a shaky but satisfactory end.

The applause, which brought smiles and blushes to the ladies' faces, allowed Jonathan to surreptitiously find a chair and pull it into the shadows. He sank onto the padded cushion. Resting his head on the high wooden back, he became vaguely conscious of Jane Munrow's raspy voice speaking some words on behalf of his proposed new water system. After each performance, it seemed, the musicians were to remind the audience why they were assembled: to raise funds for the hospital and the water project.

Jonathan shifted on his chair and closed his eyes. He alone knew that digging was already under way on an improved method of supplying the town's drinking water. A holding pond and filtration system would be fully operational by Christmas. Purification of the creek water for outlying farm use was also under contract with an engineering firm from Deer Creek. In the meantime, he thought as Jane's voice droned on, all the valley residents could do was continue to boil their water and pray the epidemic did not recur.

He let his mind wander, and the next thing he knew Ted Zabersky was tuning his violin. Madison Lander and the Vahl boy carried in Erika's harp and positioned it in the center of the room. Erika followed.

Jonathan jerked upright. His wife looked ethereal in a softly gathered dress he'd never seen before. She twirled the harp stool to adjust the height and then seated herself.

At the first brush of her fingers across the strings, Jonathan forgot to breathe. Ted Zabersky played well, but the harpist...the harpist was an angel in a cloud of blue-striped lawn. The melody was Mendelssohn's "On Wings of Song."

Erika's heart jolted when she glimpsed Jonathan in the far corner of Tithonia Brumbaugh's spacious front parlor. All at once her fingers felt clumsy, as if the tips were covered with thick cotton. She checked her hand position—thumbs up, palms close to the strings, as Professor Zabersky had taught her—and refocused on the notes. Bending her head, she put into the music everything she felt about the man who had been her husband a little less than a month. Joy. Peace. Ecstasy. Her body felt marvelously alive at the sight of him.

She followed the violin melody Mr. Zabersky played, feeling his subtle rubato and ritardando—fine new words she had added to her expanding vocabulary. A feeling of contentment, of knowing who she was and where she belonged, flowed through her.

She risked a peek at Jonathan. Surely he would be proud of her, pleased at her first musical triumph!

The expression on her husband's face almost made her heart stop. Dark eyebrows lifted, his tanned, angular face looked puzzled, as if something unexpected had hit him squarely between the eyes. Slowly his brows descended into a troubled frown.

Jonathan stared at his wife as if he had just this moment laid eyes on her. Music poured from the harp, beautiful sounds he had never dreamed possible, touched with nuance and emotional depth.

His wife played exquisitely!

Jonathan sat as if he'd been poleaxed. Pride flared within him, so deep and hot he feared his expanding chest would pop out the remaining shirt studs. His wife, in fact, was a very fine musician!

And, he realized at that moment, his wife was more than his wife. She was someone else, as well. Someone he did not know.

An odd twinge of unease began at the back of his neck and traveled down the length of his spine. Why should this bother him? Erika belonged to him, was now mother to his child, his partner in body and in spirit.

But inside he knew there was more. Erika was...herself. A part of her—the part he watched tonight as wonder and possessiveness warred inside him—would never be defined by her marital relationship to him. Erika was much more than Mrs. Jonathan Callender.

His breath dammed inside his chest. Erika was Erika, and she would never be entirely his.

When the piece drew to a close, Erika rose and curtsied to the audience. The clapping and cheering overwhelmed her, sent the blood into her cheeks.

Mr. Zabersky gave her a beaming smile and kissed her hand. Then he spoke under his breath. "Bravo, my dear. You make an old violinist feel young."

He stepped back, and Erika's tongue turned to cornsilk. She had let Mr. Zabersky convince her to address the assembled company with a short speech, a plea for contributions for Jonathan's new hospital. Now, facing a roomful of Plum Creek townspeople, she regretted the decision right down to her toes.

She moved a single step forward and laid one hand on the harp to steady her body's trembling. "Ladies and gentlemens. Gentle*men*," she corrected. At the sound of her voice, the clapping died.

"Professor Zabersky and I very happy to play for you this evening." Her voice shook, and she paused to draw in a shallow breath. "We tonight offer our music because we need...that is, we hope you support new hospital in Plum Creek for sick people."

She shot a look at Jonathan where he sat bolt upright on Tithonia's striped damask dining chair. His mouth opened and shut as if he had started to say something and then changed his mind. His eyes shone with a curious light, but she couldn't read the expression in them. She prayed he would approve of the words she spoke on behalf of his hospital.

She pulled her gaze away and tried desperately to remember the next line of her speech.

"Never more again," she said, then immediately amended it. "Never again you must travel to hospital in a city far away. Hospital will be right here in Plum Creek, for all people."

A smattering of applause followed, and then someone called out a question. "You mean all *white* people, don'tcha, Miz Callender?"

Erika jerked. White people? What did he mean? She lifted her hand off the harp and raised her chin. "All people," she repeated. Her quiet voice sounded firm and strong in the sudden silence.

"Black folks, too?" the voice pursued. "And Injuns?"

"How 'bout that passel of Chinese behind the livery?" someone else added.

Erika felt a sudden chill sweep over the parlor. From across the room, she caught Tithonia's narrowed gaze. Her hostess would not want controversy stirred up at a social event in her home. Of course, at *no* time or place would Tithonia want even the hint of bending the old rules by which she and the

residents of Plum Creek had lived for two generations.

Erika let her glance rest on the assembled guests.
None of them wanted change. Not Tithonia, not any
of the ladies of the quilting circle, possibly not any
woman or man in all of Jackson County. Especially
if it meant the rights of a previously shunned minor-
ity would change, too.

Her breath clogged inside her lungs. What about
Jonathan?

It occurred to her she had no idea what her husband's thoughts were on the subject. She loved Jonathan, admired his dedication to healing the sick.
And yet, she realized with a rush of horror, she had
assumed his feelings would be the same as hers. Now
she acknowledged that she could not be sure of that.
She had only her own assumptions about his beliefs.

What a puzzle marriage was! How was it a woman
could know a man intimately and yet not know the
depth of his spirit?

Because, an inner voice whispered, *you see him in
your own image! And he does the same. Neither of
you really knows the other. That is the real adventure
of a marriage!*

She heard the low rumble of dissatisfaction among
the guests crowding Tithonia's parlor. Her stomach
floated up behind her rib cage and turned over.

She needed Jonathan's approval, his love. She

longed for Tithonia's acceptance, and that of the other ladies, but now an insistent idea lodged in the back of her mind.

It didn't matter what Jonathan or Tithonia or anyone else thought about black people or Indians or the Chinese families in town. She knew what *she* thought.

She recalled the elderly Negro farrier down at the livery stable, the two Chinese families who lived in a single shack and worked laying railroad track between Plum Creek and Rose City. She thought of Micah Tallhorse and his brother, the offerings of smoked fish and fresh vegetables left on the back porch steps. They were human beings, too.

She steeled her nerves and opened her lips to speak. "Yes," she acknowledged. "The hospital should be open to all the people."

A murmur ran around the room. Instantly, Tithonia heaved herself to her feet. "Next," she said in a commanding voice, "we are honored to hear Mr. Zabersky's talented daughter, Mary, and her betrothed, Mr. Whitman Vahl. They will perform for us a new song, all the way from St. Louis."

As she moved aside, Erika sought Jonathan's eyes. His steady perusal dashed her entire body in ice water. Hard-eyed and still frowning, he held her gaze for an interminable minute, and then he sent her a barely perceptible nod.

She had no idea what the gesture signified. Approval? Barely concealed toleration? Acknowledgment of battle lines drawn between them?

Her heart pounding, Erika accepted Theodore Zabersky's arm and allowed him to conduct her to a seat. She watched Madison Lander carry her harp away and tried to quiet her breathing.

Mary Zabersky took her place at the piano, and Erika forced herself to concentrate on the young woman's calm demeanor. She intended to learn as much about proper deportment as she could by studying how other ladies conducted themselves. Every social gathering was an opportunity for instruction.

Still shaking from the words she had spoken in public, she pressed her back into her chair and tried to quell the thudding of her heart.

As Mary's clear soprano voice carried the strains of "While Strolling Through the Park" over the chords strummed on Whitman's guitar, Erika fancied Jonathan's eyes on her, boring into her back.

She had made a mistake, a terrible mistake. She had spoken out on an unpopular issue, damaged Jonathan's chances for hospital donations. Oh, why could she never just *think* things and not speak them out in words?

She longed to escape the hot, crowded room, longed to remove her tight, buttoned shoes and run barefooted through the cool grass in the town square. She was a peasant at heart. Too simple in her tastes and too outspoken in her opinions to be a fine lady.

Or, she admitted with a sinking feeling inside her belly, a doctor's wife.

It had been a mistake to marry Jonathan. She had reached for happiness, for marriage with a man she admired and loved, but she knew now that she could never live up to its obligations.

Linda Ladd   260

Chapter Twenty

"I finished icing my orange cake," Mrs. Benbow said from the kitchen stove. "I'm just puttin' the roast into the oven, so why don't you lie down and take a bit of a rest, lass? You look all tired out."

Erika was in a fizz of nerves. It was her first dinner party, and Jonathan had been called out to the Rukavin place. With pure terror, she faced the prospect of entertaining the mayor and his wife on her own.

The occasion was a celebration of two events—Plotinus and Tithonia Brumbaugh's thirty-second wedding anniversary and release of the last cholera patient from Jonathan's hospital. After six long weeks, the epidemic appeared to be over.

At Jonathan's suggestion, Erika had invited Theodore Zabersky and his daughter, Mary, together with Mary's fiancé, Whitman Vahl, Gwen Shaunessey and her elderly mother, Mrs. Madsen. Try as she might, Erika could not calm her nerves, and here it was the afternoon of the affair!

She would be a failure as a hostess. If it weren't for Mrs. Benbow's menu advice and solicitous guidance through the pitfalls of planning her first at-home social event, Erika would have crept out to the backyard hours ago and poured out her fears to Jasmine, the goat.

"Yes, I—oh! Not yet. I forget flowers for table. *The* table," she corrected. She flitted out to the laundry porch, then dashed back into the kitchen for the flower shears she kept hanging near the back door.

"Iris and…and…" Her mind went blank. What sort of flowers were proper for the dining table? Valerian blooms had too sharp a scent, and besides, they were carmine red. She liked close color combinations, but Tithonia had once remarked that Erika's front garden beds looked "mixed up."

Since then, Erika had walked the streets of Plum Creek and studied the gardens of other houses. Roses, mostly. Tiny pink ones or floppy, fragrant yellow blooms arched over trellises.

She had no rosebushes. Maybe next year, she vowed. She would ask for cuttings and plant them blended together in related shades, like a tapestry.

In her mind, she began to lay out the garden beds as she marched up and down the path, shears in hand.

She'd give anything to be able to kneel and dig in the rich dirt instead of entertaining seven people at dinner!

She gathered all the purple iris stalks in bloom, then glanced at the swaths of black-eyed Susans she'd planted against the foundation. Yes! Quickly she cut a huge armload.

When the hall clock struck six, the baby was fed and changed and put to bed, the mouthwatering smell of Mrs. Benbow's rosemary-encrusted roast drifted upstairs, and her yellow-striped taffeta evening gown lay on her bed, freshly pressed. Even though she spent the nights with Jonathan in the master bedroom, she still used her small bedroom as a private retreat and dressing room.

By six-thirty, Jonathan had still not returned home, and their guests were due at seven. Erika peered out the window at the waning light. Had he been delayed by something unexpected at the Rukavins'? Stopped to visit another farm along the way or perhaps developed one of his headaches?

He couldn't have forgotten! She'd spent too many sleepless nights confiding to him her fears about the upcoming dinner gathering for him to be unmindful of the date.

Her fingers fumbled with the corset lacings as the feeling of foreboding grew stronger. Something was going to happen tonight, she could feel it in her bones. Mama had always said she could often sense a disaster before it happened.

A headache of her own nagged at the back of her head, and her mouth suddenly felt dry. *Jonathan wouldn't leave me to do this alone, would he? As punishment for speaking out at the recital?*

Not one word had passed his lips about that evening. Other than gripping her arm so tightly it hurt and hustling her home to bed and a night of lovemaking that still made her blush, Jonathan had never revealed how he felt about her outspoken opinions. Or about the proposed hospital's admittance policy. Since the recital, she hadn't had the courage to ask him. Some instinct told her to leave well enough alone. For now, anyway.

She drew on the cool, silky material of her new evening dress. Oh, so extravagant! Jonathan had showered her with gifts: parasols and shoes and gowns, two paisley shawls, a black velvet cape. Once she protested that all she really needed was a plain denim work skirt because her old one was worn out, and he had bought her three new ones—not denim, but sateen in beautiful colors like rose and forest green and blue.

She adjusted the short puffed sleeves and low-cut neckline of her dress, then turned to the framed mirror on the dresser. Looking back at her was someone she didn't recognize.

Her cheeks were flushed from the heat of the kitchen where she'd helped Mrs. Benbow peel potatoes and slice carrots for the past hour. Her eyes shone with a hot inner light. She looked feverish, overexcited.

"Never again," she swore aloud. "Never again a party dinner for Missus Mayor or anyone else!" She preferred to eat her meals in the company of Jonathan or at the cozy kitchen table with Mrs. Benbow.

Still, she wanted to please Jonathan, yearned to step into the role of doctor's wife with ease and flair the way his former wife would have. She knew Tess had been trained from birth in the ways of proper social conduct; Erika had learned everything from scratch. Underneath, she would never feel comfortable.

She looked down at her feet, encased in supple French kid dress slippers. *Stadtschue,* Mama would have called them. City shoes. Her toes felt mashed under the black leather. She would never learn to like such contraptions!

She swallowed hard and headed for the stairs. When the doorbell sounded in the front hall, her throat tightened. *So soon?* And Jonathan was not here yet!

Mrs. Benbow, resplendent in a new lace-trimmed black bombazine dress, opened the door.

Tithonia swept past the housekeeper in a flurry of

lilac ruffles and pleats. "Erika, my dear!" the mayor's wife gushed. A waterfall of purple lace trembled over the older woman's ample bosom.

Plotinus tagged at her elbow. The plump mayor lifted his stiff straw hat and handed it to Mrs. Benbow, then loosened the buttons on his double-breasted frock coat and turned to Erika.

"Don't mind tellin' you, Miz Callender, it's a warm night for a suit, even a linen one!"

Erika smiled and pressed his hand. The mayor and his wife were early! *Oh, God, help me to think! What am I supposed to do?*

"Jonathan n-not home yet," Erika stammered. "Other guests not arrived yet, so please, come into parlor."

Tithonia embraced her. "We'll just entertain ourselves, then, won't we?" She linked arms with Erika and drew her toward the parlor doorway.

Out of the corner of her eye she saw Mrs. Benbow direct a sharp-eyed look at the mayor's wife. "Dinner'll be at seven, like the invitation said," the housekeeper snapped. "My roast needs a spell to set and—"

Tithonia ignored her. "Naturally. Come along, Erika. You must show me some new song on your harp. Professor Zabersky, he taught my Jenny, you know. Such a capable man! He tells me you're quite the brightest light among his pupils."

Erika gaped at her. She was not prepared to play this evening. She had barely recovered from her performance nerves the night of Tithonia's charity recital.

Too late she realized that of course she would be expected to play! Ladies always entertained their guests; that's why they took lessons and practiced—to be "accomplished."

She was unprepared for the ordeal. The only thing she could play was the accompaniment for Mr. Zabersky's violin piece, but just the arpeggiated chords alone amounted to...to nothing!

"Oh, but I—" She broke off in midsentence. She would *not* be bullied by Tithonia. And certainly not in her own house! A wave of dizziness washed over her at the audacity of what she was about to do, but she shook her head to clear it and straightened her spine.

"We will perform tonight, Mrs. Brumbaugh, but it will be a surprise for you and the mayor. For anniversary."

Tithonia sent her a delighted look and turned to her husband. "Oh, Tiny, do you hear that? A surprise! You know how I love surprises!"

The mayor patted her shoulder. "My dear, that I do. I wonder what our hostess has planned!"

Erika blanched. She, herself, wondered exactly the same thing!

The Zaberskys arrived next, Mary in a soft brocaded rose silk, holding tight to Whitman Vahl's hand and blushing, her father looking stiff and elegant in a formal frock coat and black top hat. When Gwen Shaunessey and Mrs. Madsen appeared, Erika conducted them to the parlor, then went to help Mrs. Benbow in the kitchen while the guests chatted.

Just when the housekeeper declared her roast couldn't wait one more minute before serving, Jonathan burst in through the back door.

"I am sorry to be so late, Erika, on this night of all nights, but—" He closed his arm around her shoulders and hugged her, careful not to let his dusty jacket touch her gown. "I went to see Samuel Tallhorse. Micah found me at the Rukavin place. Said his brother's leg was stiffening. I rode out to the reservation to check on it."

Erika nodded. He smelled of horse and sweat and dust. At the moment, she wished her husband was a banker like Plotinus Brumbaugh, with regular hours and a predictable life.

"Can you bathe and change in—" she cast a questioning look at Mrs. Benbow, poised over the roast with a carving knife in her hand "—ten minutes?"

"I can. I'll carve that at the table, Mrs. Benbow." He planted a quick kiss on Erika's warm cheek. "Ten minutes," he promised. And he was gone, sneaking upstairs on cat feet while Erika rejoined her guests.

"My husband was called away," she explained. "To the reservation. He is dressing now and soon will join us."

She went on struggling to make conversation for minute upon agonizing minute, waiting for Jonathan to appear. Finally, when she had exhausted her studiously practiced list of small-talk phrases, she lapsed into uneasy silence.

She was sure her head would explode from the strain of entertaining a roomful of people all by herself. How could she have been so foolish as to think she could ever play the role of a lady? She smiled at Gwen Shaunessey, encouraging her to continue the story she was telling, forcing herself to concentrate so she could ask polite questions later.

At last Jonathan appeared in the doorway.

Tall and handsome in a dark suit with a gray silk tie knotted at his throat, her husband advanced among the guests, shaking hands and grinning as if nothing untoward had happened. Erika was so glad to see him she could have wept.

The gray silk exactly matched his eyes, she noted. When he paused before her, took her hands in his and held them to his lips, her heart soared. She was his, body and soul, and—wanton that she was—she delighted in it.

"Ladies, gentlemen," he announced with an engaging smile. "I believe dinner is served."

As the meal began, Erika looked to Mrs. Benbow for subtle guidance in pacing the courses. Soup came first, tomato bisque flavored with fresh basil. Then a salad of chilled asparagus spears on beds of watercress, and finally slices of succulent roast beef with browned potatoes and carrots.

She could not taste a thing. Lumps of food went down her throat like so much paste. Jonathan poured wine and made easy, amiable conversation with Tithonia on his right and Mary Zabersky on his left, then methodically progressed down one side of the long table and up the other, drawing each guest out, sharing anecdotes, playing the perfect host.

Erika studied him as the main course progressed, tried to emulate his conversational technique with Plotinus on her right. Mrs. Benbow sat just to her left, occasionally intoning a word or two of guidance but otherwise eating in silence.

Laughter and the sound of clinking glassware faded as she stared at her husband's chiseled features, watched his purposeful hands lift a knife, tip a glass to his lips. Her head spun.

Plotinus leaned forward over his laden china plate. "Out at the Indian reservation tonight, were you, Jon? Any trouble?"

"No trouble," Jonathan replied. "Just a broken

leg I set a while back. I'll have to reset it. It's healed crooked.''

Tithonia set her fork down with a clank. "Where will you do this. In town?"

Jonathan looked up. "Yes, in town. I have to re-break the bone, under ether, of course. I'll do it at the hospital, since there are no cholera cases left."

Tithonia's lace waterfall fluttered. "I'm sure the *new* hospital, when we raise sufficient funds to construct it, will not accept Indians."

"Why not?" Erika heard herself blurt out.

Tithonia's jaw snapped shut.

"Because, my dear," Plotinus said, patting Erika's hand, "we expect any, er, project my wife and I support, uh, contribute money to, must meet with Tith—with our...um...approval."

Erika caught Jonathan's steady gaze. She knew he hoped for the mayor's financial backing for both the hospital and the new water system. And the Brumbaughs were guests in their home. She must not insult them.

But it was wrong, what Tithonia and the mayor said. *Wrong!* No one who was sick or in need should be excluded because of his heritage. She held her husband's glance across the table, tried to read his feelings. How she longed to see into his heart!

But Jonathan adroitly shifted the subject, and again conversation swirled around her. Mrs. Benbow signaled it was time for dessert, and Erika rose to help the older woman clear away the dinner plates.

"It's unusual, to say the least." Tithonia's voice followed Erika into the quiet haven of the kitchen. She leaned her head against the shelf of kettles near the stove and shut her eyes. How could she even *think* she could entertain like a lady? It took all her resolve to keep from fleeing through the laundry porch and outside where Jasmine was tied under the plum tree.

But she would not. Could not. Only cowards ran away.

Erika reentered the dining room bearing the layered orange cake on a plate in time to hear Tithonia's final words.

"I always supposed household help should remain in the kitchen during a meal, not sit at the same table with the guests. Isn't that so, Jon?"

Erika clattered the cake plate down in front of her place and bit her lip so hard she tasted blood. She would ignore the rude remark. She would cut the slices while Mrs. Benbow passed dessert plates. *She would smile and she would mind her tongue!*

Holding her breath, she waited for Jonathan's reply.

"Perfectly so, Tithonia. In all houses but this one."

"Personally, don't you feel your wife could be taught to manage the serving so..."

Erika slapped down the cake knife, glad the housekeeper was in the kitchen, out of hearing.

"Mrs. Benbow," she said, her voice quiet but determined, "is a valued member of my husband's household. She is not servant. And," she added with calm conviction, "she is also a friend. Here, now, is Mrs. Benbow with the coffee. Missus Mayor, do you take cream or sugar?"

Jonathan's gaze was unreadable, but she did notice that when his cup had been filled, he lifted it in a subtle salute before he put it to his lips.

She must bite her tongue for the rest of the evening. For the rest of her life! No matter how provoking Tithonia could be, Erika knew she could not, would not, allow herself to be drawn into a debate with a guest in her house. She resolved she would get through the next two hours—and the surprise for Tithonia and Plotinus's anniversary—by acting the part of a lady. A well-mannered society lady.

No matter what.

Mrs. Benbow resumed her seat, passed the dessert plates and poured coffee. If she had heard anything from the kitchen, she gave no indication.

Choking down the thick feeling in her throat, Erika smiled at her dinner guests and forked a bite of the tangy orange cake into her parched mouth. *I will survive this night. Survive and triumph.*

Her only fear was that Jonathan would not approve of the next part of her plan.

Chapter Twenty-One

All during dinner Erika fretted silently over how to entertain her guests in some ladylike musical fashion. But what should she do? She didn't play the harp well enough to improvise a song, but she would be expected to do *something*.

The fleeting idea that had come to her earlier seemed like a childhood fantasy, but it kept recurring, and finally Erika set her mind to using it. By the time she had eaten half her portion of Mrs. Benbow's delicious orange layer cake, she had decided what she would do. She prayed Jonathan would understand.

"Now," chirped Tithonia as she polished off the last crumb of the generous slice of cake Erika had served her, "do tell us, Erika, what is this surprise you promised?"

Erika managed a shaky smile. Jonathan's half puzzled, half bemused expression gave her pause, but in the next instant she reviewed her options and stiffened her resolve.

She had no choice, really, but to try to carry it off as if she'd planned it weeks ago. Tithonia and the other guests expected entertainment in addition to dinner. Even though the prospect had caught Erika off guard, in the homes of proper ladies such things were taken for granted, and she would approach the challenge as a test of her—what was the new word she'd learned last night? Ingenuity, that was it! She hoped Jonathan would view it in the same vein. Entertainment her guests would certainly get!

"Well," Tithonia inquired in a voice breathless with anticipation. "What may we expect?"

"And when," echoed Gwen Shaunessey. "Soon, I hope. Mama tends to nod off after meals." She smiled at Mrs. Madsen seated across from her. "Unless she is kept amused."

Erika cleared her throat. "Then we will begin. First, will need a sugar bowl, an empty one. And a piece of writing paper."

Jonathan rose instantly, strode into his study and returned with a sheet of his engraved stationery. Dumping the scant remains of the sugar bowl onto his dessert plate, he handed both bowl and paper to his wife.

He hadn't the foggiest notion what she had in

mind, but he was intrigued in spite of himself. In fact, intrigued didn't half describe his interest. Fascinated was more like it! He'd had no idea Erika had planned some additional entertainment for this evening. A most surprising woman he had married!

He glanced down the length of the table, watched Erika return her coffee cup to its saucer and begin to methodically tear his stationery into squares with slim, capable fingers.

"A pencil, Jonathan?"

He produced one immediately from his inner coat pocket, passed it to Mary Zabersky, who handed it to her betrothed and on down to Erika at the opposite end of the table. While Mrs. Benbow cleared away the dessert plates, Erika wrote something on each slip of paper, folded it once and dropped it into the empty sugar bowl.

She shook the contents of the bowl with childish pleasure, and Jonathan hid a smile.

"In Schleswig, where I grow up, is child's game for birthday," his wife explained. "Here—" she held up the bowl "—is for drawing partners for entertaining."

Tithonia clapped her hands with glee. "My dear, what a perfectly wonderful idea!" Plotinus bobbed his head in agreement, and the others burst into excited talk. Even Mrs. Madsen perked up. Mary Zabersky and Whitman Vahl hugged each other.

"Oh, quick," Tithonia said in a breathless voice. "Do tell us, how does the game work?"

Erika rose, the sugar bowl in her hands. "First, each person draws a name for partner. When all names are drawn, then have fifteen minutes to decide what to present. Can sing or recite or dance or...what you like. Then—" she paused for dramatic effect "—we perform for each other! Is fun!"

Her enthusiasm carried even Mrs. Madsen along on a wave of excitement. The old lady beamed when allowed to pick first, and when she drew Jonathan's name, she fanned herself with coquettish charm.

Jonathan suppressed a groan. How in the name of all the saints could he and the frail old woman come up with anything even halfway amusing? He watched in envy as Ted Zabersky drew Adeline Benbow as his partner. At least Adeline could sing, and Ted was as accomplished on the harmonica as he was on the violin.

Tithonia's lashes fluttered when she was paired with Whitman Vahl, leaving Mary Zabersky to team with Gwen. By default, Erika was partnered with Plotinus Brumbaugh.

Before Erika could open her mouth for further instructions, the teams scattered to various parts of the house to prepare. Gwen and Mary made a beeline for the kitchen. Ted Zabersky moved his chair closer to Adeline Benbow's and gallantly filled her cup from the coffee server. Tithonia collared the young Vahl boy and headed for the parlor, leaving Erika and Plotinus in the main hall.

It was a brilliant scheme, Jonathan thought. By Christmas it would be the rage at social gatherings all over the valley. He himself hadn't felt such anticipation since he was a child in Philadelphia.

A twinge of regret nibbled at his delight in his wife's unusual capabilities. Even with her unique approach to after-dinner entertainment, Erika had unknowingly finessed herself into a corner. Her partner, Plotinus Brumbaugh, was completely tone-deaf!

With a flourishy bow, he escorted Mrs. Madsen into his study and closed the door, his thoughts still on Erika. She had managed the dinner beautifully, conversed and poured coffee like any young woman of society. And she looked enchanting in that yellow taffeta with her golden hair braided into a crown on top of her head.

But what a source of the unexpected she was! He sighed in perplexed happiness. True, he was proud of her. Even when he didn't understand her, couldn't fathom why she resolutely continued to nurture parts of her daily life that had nothing to do with him, he admired her, nonetheless.

At Mrs. Madsen's discreet cough, Jonathan jerked his attention back to the matter at hand.

* * *

At exactly nine o'clock Erika tapped on the study door. "Time is up," she called.

The others had already gathered in the front parlor when Jonathan and Mrs. Madsen joined them. He prayed fervently they would be selected to perform first. The old lady grew more drowsy with each passing minute. She had to stay awake for her part in their presentation.

Erika *shhed* for quiet. "Our guests of honor, Missus and Mayor Brumbaugh, may now command the performers." She resumed her seat to the rustle of excited whispering.

Jonathan found he couldn't take his eyes off his wife. What a surprising woman, he thought again. However, her independent tendencies left him shaking his head in frustration. It was not at all how one's wife *should* be. And yet, "should" didn't seem to apply to Erika. She was herself first and his wife second. A new breed of woman, he recognized. One that he instinctively distrusted.

It was impossible to dislike Erika, especially at times like tonight. He knew she had worried for long hours, worked hard to make this occasion a success. And she looked so lovely doing it. Still, he acknowledged as he watched her graciously turn the festivities over to Tithonia and Plotinus, a man wanted his wife to belong to him, to be at his side, in his home, not off on her own doing God only knew what.

It was selfish of him, he admitted. But he was the breadwinner of the household. It was he who practiced a profession. Erika needed nothing beyond what he could provide for her.

Did she?

Again the uneasy thought came. *Perhaps I am not enough for her.*

"Jonathan and Mrs. Madsen will go first," Tithonia proclaimed.

Jonathan heaved a quiet sigh of relief, set aside his wandering thoughts and offered Mrs. Madsen his arm. Together they turned to face their audience.

"'Once upon a midnight dreary,'" Jonathan began to recite, "'while I pondered, weak and weary...'" When he came to "Quoth the raven," he stopped dramatically.

Slowly Mrs. Madsen opened her thin lips and croaked a single word. "'Nevermore.'"

As they continued the poem, even Jonathan was astonished at the dramatic variety the old lady conjured up for her repeated one-word utterance. When they concluded, Tithonia was so delighted she called for an encore, but Jonathan tactfully declined. Mrs. Madsen was fading fast.

Mary and Gwen Shaunessey sang three verses of "Grandfather's Clock" from memory, and Adeline Benbow and Ted Zabersky stunned everyone by dancing an energetic Scottish jig while the onlookers

clapped time. Tithonia then persuaded Whitman Vahl
to play musical selections on Mr. Zabersky's harmonica both before and after her lengthy and spirited
rendition of "The Solitary Reaper."

Jonathan tried not to chuckle at young Whitman's
musical choices: "Listen to the Mockingbird," and
"Nobody Knows the Trouble I've Seen." He'd bet
Tithonia missed the irony.

Then it was Erika's turn. Jonathan held his breath
as she took her place at the harp and nodded at her
partner.

Plotinus inhaled deeply, and Erika strummed a single chord.

"'Friends, Romans, countrymen,'" the mayor bel-
lowed.

Another chord.

Plotinus raised a clenched fist. "'Lend me your
ears!'" It went on in the same vein, the mayor reciting the passage and Erika providing simple accompaniment, like a medieval troubadour. It was surpris-
ingly effective.

How, Jonathan wondered, had she devised such
clever utilization of a man who could not sing a single note?

She ended Plotinus's Shakespeare reading with a
rippling arpeggio, one he had heard her practice with
painstaking care for weeks before the charity recital.

Erika raised her head and smiled at her guests. Her

eyes glowed with an odd look, and suddenly Jonathan studied her more closely. Her cheeks flamed, but the skin of her forehead and neck looked pale and moist. She looked fragile. Disoriented.

Something was wrong.

He moved forward, held out his arms. Erika took a single step toward him, lifted one shaking hand to her temple and collapsed.

Chapter Twenty-Two

Cholera.

Jonathan leaned his forehead against the white-painted windowsill in Erika's tiny bedroom. He rebelled at accepting his own diagnosis, but the symptoms were unmistakable. *God in heaven, why now?* Why, when the epidemic he'd fought for endless, heartbreaking weeks was finally waning?

And oh, God, why Erika? At his request, she had even boiled her bathwater to destroy the deadly bacillus. Unless...

Cold sweat soaked the shirt between his shoulder blades. Unless she had contracted the disease by touching something or someone already contaminated. The butcher's counter. A doorknob in someone's home. Those in his own house were disinfected daily by Mrs. Benbow, but Erika often left the house, went out in the afternoon to Valey's Mercantile, to help at church socials, on errands for Mrs. Benbow.

He resented her every absence, even her attendance at Sunday evening Methodist Church services. Maybe she had touched someone's unwashed hand, a soiled hymnal.

For the tenth time in the past hour he felt for her pulse. Under his fingers her shallow heartbeat was irregular and more rapid than the last time.

She'd vomited all night, fought off her blankets. He brought the teaspoon of salted water to her lips, but she twisted her head away. He held her chin and tried to force the fluid into her mouth.

She would die if he couldn't hydrate her cramp-racked body. It wasn't the bacillus that took cholera victims, but the debilitating dehydration. The heart weakened and eventually failed. Once cholera struck, even young, strong bodies like Erika's succumbed.

Why could she not have remained at home, where she was safe? Of course, that was unreasonable. No woman deserved to be imprisoned in her house, even for her own protection. His rational mind acknowledged that truth, but at the same time his gut-level emotions willed it otherwise. Any man in his right mind wanted his wife at home, safe, did he not? Not flying about town on mysterious, possibly dangerous, missions of her own.

Good Lord, if he heard himself utter such thoughts

out loud he'd judge that he'd gone mad! The possessiveness he recognized in himself since Erika had come into his life he would not tolerate in another man. But Erika...his Erika...

He might lose her. His heart turned to ice at the thought. Mrs. Benbow brought another basin of cool water. He bathed Erika's face and neck, dipping the soft cloth often and wringing it out with hands he could barely control they shook so violently. Her skin felt hot and sticky.

"I've taken the babe down to my own room," the housekeeper said. "It'll be safer for the child, and quieter for Erika."

"Yes, Adeline. Thank you." He dipped the cloth again.

"And I'm praying, Jon. You should, too."

He couldn't answer. He bowed his head and tried to form some words, but they slid into a fog before he could grasp their meaning.

All night he had sat at Erika's bedside, watching her writhe in the grip of the debilitating fever. He'd left her only long enough to milk the goat for the baby's breakfast.

In the morning Erika was worse. By afternoon, she had slipped into a stupor.

Mrs. Benbow tramped heavily up the stairs. "Saw Tithonia at the service tonight. Prayer vigils are being held at both the Presbyterian and the Methodist churches.''

Jonathan bowed his head, his eyes burning.

Rutherford Chilcoate delivered a quart of his latest elixir formula, along with a note. ''No spirits, just sarsaparilla and peppermint leaves. Two tablespoons every hour.''

Jonathan used every drop.

Tithonia paid a brief call. ''My persimmons have come on, so I made up a batch of my persimmon tea. You will try it, won't you?''

He tried it. Erika couldn't swallow. Her heartbeat jumped and fluttered, no stronger than leaves rustled by the wind.

On the third day Micah Tallhorse appeared on the back porch, a deerskin packet in his hand. He thrust it toward Jonathan. ''She drink. Make sweat.''

Jonathan folded back the corners and sniffed the dried herbs. He clasped the Indian's hand and found he could not speak.

Micah nodded. ''Bring more tonight. Medicine maker must say words over.''

A hot, swollen feeling choked Jonathan's throat. He had great respect for Indian remedies, but what Erika needed was a miracle, not just an herbal drink. Nevertheless, when he reentered the kitchen, he set the teakettle on the stove.

By evening, he knew she was dying. She had

drunk and sweated and still her heartbeat faltered. Her few words, spoken in delirium, jumbled together in Jonathan's mind, mixed up with his own incoherent snatches of prayer.

The faint sound of a church choir drifted through the open window. "'Amazing grace, how sweet the sound....'"

Downstairs, Mrs. Benbow stood at the stove sobbing as she heated the baby's milk.

Ted Zabersky brought an armload of white roses and stood on the veranda, unsure what to say, until Jonathan appeared. Overcome, the old gentleman thrust the flowers into the doctor's hands without a word, and Mrs. Benbow led the shaken man away to the kitchen for a cup of strong tea.

Jonathan mounted the stairs and spilled the roses at the foot of Erika's bed. Their sweet vanilla scent filled the room.

Midnight came. In the dark, silent house the hall clock struck the hours with ominous regularity. *The earth turns,* Jonathan thought. *The sun rises and sets, some are born, and some...*

His mind was so tired he felt numb. Detached. He sat for another hour listening to Erika's erratic breathing, sponging her face and arms with cool water and watching the round, gold moon float outside the window. God in His mercy would not let her suffer much longer.

Two o'clock. Three. The hour when every physician knew death stalked the weak. Soon. It would be soon.

Suddenly he wanted to talk to her. "Erika," he murmured. "Erika, listen to me."

She moaned, her legs scrabbling under the blankets.

"Listen, my darling. I wanted to keep you..." His voice choked off, and he fought for control. "To keep you safe. I wanted nothing to ever hurt you or make you unhappy. But I failed. I couldn't protect you from life, my dearest. I know now that you wouldn't have wanted me to, but I would gladly give my own..."

He stopped to steady his voice. "I want...want you to know how much..." His voice broke. He smoothed the tendrils of hair from her forehead and waited until he could speak.

"Oh, my darling girl, you have taught me so much. Only now am I beginning to learn what love is, and—"

He drew in an uneven breath. "Oh, God, Erika. I don't want you to die! I want you to stay here on earth with me. And our daughter. I want you to go on playing your harp and taking pies to those interminable church bazaars. I want you to tell Tithonia Brumbaugh to mind her own business! I want whatever you want, my darling. Just come back. *Come back.*"

Her breath rattled in, out. In again. He couldn't stand watching her struggle. He had to do something to ease her suffering.

The harp. She would want to hear the harp.

He eased off the bed and moved to the doorway. Down the stairs to the front parlor where the instrument stood silhouetted against the wall in the moonlight. He yanked it into his grip and muscled it to the bottom of the staircase.

He went up the stairs backward, taking a single step at a time and dragging the harp over each carpeted riser. He made slow, thumping progress, and he didn't dare stop to rest.

The clock struck four. God would take her soon.

Chapter Twenty-Three

Jonathan pulled the harp to Erika's bedside and brushed his fingers over the strings. The silvery sound bloomed and faded. He strummed it again, more slowly, made the sound last longer. The notes shimmered in the still room, bringing an odd sense of peace.

Gently he sat down beside his wife and tipped the harp onto his shoulder as he had seen her do. He plucked a single string, then another. The ethereal sounds fed his ravaged soul. He prayed they would ease her passage.

He played notes at random, letting an inner spirit guide him. A minute, an hour, he didn't know. Time had no meaning anymore. All he knew was that he had to reach her, had to be with her at the end. Such intangible gifts were the only things that mattered in life.

He felt something rip inside his chest, and suddenly time seemed to slow. What mattered was that he loved Erika, just as she was—caring, industrious, independent-minded, annoyingly outspoken. She was herself. An original. He did not need to understand her, he needed only to love her.

A weight lifted from his heart. It was all clear now. He loved Erika, but he did not own her. She would never belong to him in that sense, and it no longer mattered. Erika would belong to him because she freely chose to spend her life—her frustratingly independent life—with him.

His fingers stilled on the strings, and he felt Erika stir beside him.

"Jonathan?"

He started at the sound of her voice. "Erika? Can you hear me?"

"Jonathan?" she murmured again. "Hold me."

He released the harp and gathered her close. "Erika," he whispered. "Erika." She smelled faintly of vanilla.

Quickly he felt for her pulse, rested his palm on her brow. He must be dreaming. Hallucinating, even. Her skin felt cool and dry. Her heart thumped against his chest.

"Erika, are you in pain? Do your legs hurt? Your stomach?"

She was silent for a long moment. "No. But I am thirsty."

Thirsty! She was thirsty? *She was thirsty!* Next she would be hungry, and then...

He wrapped his arms tight about her. *God in heaven! His wife was warm and alive in his arms.*

He pressed his face into her hair and wept.

By Christmas Eve, Erika was well enough to attend the debut of Tithonia Brumbaugh's new Dramatic Arts Society, followed by supper and dancing. Bundled in a thick fur robe, Erika allowed Jonathan to fuss and hover over her. She didn't need such cosseting, but she knew it made him happy.

She had been wheeling Marian Elizabeth's baby carriage to Valey's Mercantile and back for a week now; she had just not told Jonathan. Since he was out on calls or closeted in his study with patients most of the daylight hours, he rarely noticed her absences. Besides, walking was good for her now.

Tithonia's dramatic presentations were highlighted by a pageant depicting scenes from *Ivanhoe*. Erika thought she recognized the draperies she had donated to the Methodist church bazaar in October, but she couldn't be sure. Royal blue and crimson dye covered the identifying damask rose pattern.

Privately she thought Tithonia a little buxom as Rowena, but dark-haired Susan Ransom was an elegant Rebecca, and Plotinus played the Templar knight to perfection.

When the final act was over, Jonathan leaned toward her. "Would you like to go home now and rest?"

"No," she whispered. "Now we will have dancing and after that the Presbyterian ladies are to serve supper."

Scarcely able to believe his ears, Jonathan stared at her. "I thought you didn't enjoy dancing, Erika? At our wedding, as I recall, you preferred brandy to waltzes."

His teasing tone masked his surprise. He would never be able to keep up with Erika. Never.

"I have learned much since then," she said. "I like now the dancing. With you," she murmured. "I like very much."

A shy smile touched her lips, and his heart constricted.

"I ask you, Jonathan. Dance me."

Jonathan shook his head to clear the cobwebs from his brain. He was sure a deeper meaning was attached to her words. "It's not dancing we're talking about, is it?"

She turned a speculative gaze on him. "No. Is not." She rose, stretched her arms to his shoulders. "Please. Dance me. I want to be close with you."

Jonathan stood up. "Yes," he said in a voice shaking with emotion. "I will dance you. Any time, any place you say. For the rest of my life."

She moved into his arms. "Jonathan," she murmured against his cheek. "You will remember, I...warm easy."

For a moment his brain went blank. *I warm easy?* What was she really telling him?

He stared down into his wife's luminous blue eyes, and the answer came in a flash. She meant for him not to crush her own life, her own self. Not to keep her spirit imprisoned in the large gray house on Maple Street. That's what she'd wanted him to understand all along.

"Yes, my darling, I remember."

She settled her slim hand on his shoulder. "Then we will begin," she whispered. "Dance me..."

He caught her in his arms. Their voices blended as they spoke together one final word.

"Loose."

Epilogue

In the spring, Brumbaugh Hospital admitted its first patient when eleven-year-old Sally Sinclair broke her collarbone playing Ivanhoe in a tournament with the Rukavin boys.

Rutherford Waterworks elected Jonathan Callender chairman of the board and Rutherford Chilcoate as executive director.

In June, Whitman Vahl married Mary Zabersky in the rose arbor at her father's home. Erika and Mr. Zabersky performed during the garden reception.

The following Sunday at the Presbyterian church, Theodore Zabersky claimed Adeline Benbow as his bride.

Two weeks later, on a day when the cloudless sky arched like a blue bowl over Plum Creek, Erika Callender gave birth to a baby girl. They named her Jonna Adeline.

That evening, through the lighted windows of the large gray house on Maple Street, Dr. Jonathan Callender could be seen lifting his wife in his arms and slowly turning around and around in the graceful steps of a waltz.

* * * * *

Author Note

It is a popular myth that women of the West, particularly those in towns and cities, were delicate creatures who hid themselves away keeping house and raising families. Women of all ages and walks of life were one of the most stabilizing, civilizing elements of nineteenth-century American society, contributing their time, organizational ability and creative talents to numerous projects of educational, cultural, social and political importance.

Tight-laced corsets, bustles, starched petticoats and feathered hats did not prevent our intrepid grandmothers and great-grandmothers from rolling up their sleeves and polishing whatever part of the West they found themselves in. To such women we owe an incalculable debt of gratitude for a heritage of vision and courage.

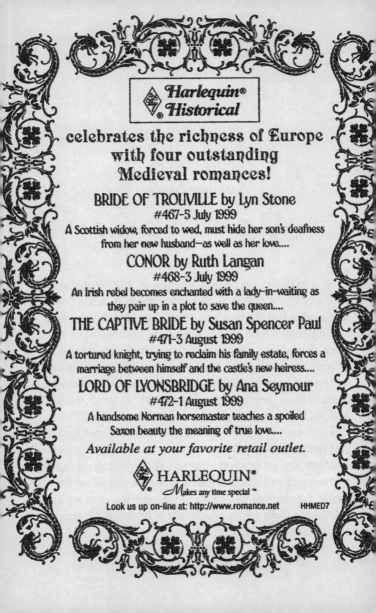

 HARLEQUIN®

Makes any time special ™

In celebration of Harlequin®'s golden anniversary

Enter to win a *dream!* You could win:

- A luxurious trip for two to *The Renaissance Cottonwoods Resort* in Scottsdale, Arizona, or

- A bouquet of flowers once a week for a year from **FTD**, or

- A $500 shopping spree, or

- A fabulous bath & body gift basket, including **K-tel**'s *Candlelight and Romance* 5-CD set.

Look for **WIN A DREAM** flash on specially marked Harlequin® titles by Penny Jordan, Dallas Schulze, Anne Stuart and Kristine Rolofson in October 1999*.

FTD

RENAISSANCE.
COTTONWOODS RESORT
SCOTTSDALE, ARIZONA

K·TEL

Celebrate **15** years with